DEATH'S TALLY

Oil and bullets — Sanderson City has swallowed plenty of both. When Walt Slade arrives to put a lid on the violence, the town is set to blow sky-high in his face. A lit fuse, a shotgun blast in the dark . . . and the ace undercover Texas Ranger is plunged into a searing sixgun showdown with a greed-crazed pack of killers.

BRADFORD SCOTT

DEATH'S TALLY

Complete and Unabridged

LINFORD
Leicester

First published in the United States by
Pyramid Books

First Linford Edition
published 2021
by arrangement with
Golden West Literary Agency

A catalogue record for this book is available
from the British Library.

ISBN 978–1–78541–957–7

Published by
Ulverscroft Limited
Anstey, Leicestershire

Printed and bound in Great Britain by
TJ Books Ltd., Padstow, Cornwall

This book is printed on acid-free paper

1

Sanderson was burned by the sun, pounded by the occasional storms of rain. Its prevailing headgear was the 'J.B.,' as the cowhands called the J. B. Stetson hat.

A railroad repair and crew change point with large shops and yards, Sanderson exported sheep, cattle, wool, mohair, and outlaws.

The outlaws were not exactly the home-grown variety, anent Sanderson, but the railroad town was a favorite stopping-off point for gentlemen with change-the-wealth notions who roamed the mountains and canyons of the Big Bend country to the southwest and, among other things, frowned upon law-enforcement officers, trafficked in 'wet' herds stolen from the great ranches in Mexico and driven across the Rio Grande and equally wet cattle stolen in Texas and driven across the river to the

Mexican buyers. The outlaws played no favorites; all was grist for their mill.

They made a habit of spending much of their ill-gotten gains in Sanderson, because of which they were tolerated by merchants and others so long as they behaved themselves in town and left their shenanigans behind. Perhaps not exactly ethical, but so wags the world.

Ranger Walt Slade, named by the *peónes* of the Rio Grande river villages *El Halcón* — The Hawk — was thinking of such mundane matters as he rounded a little knoll and skirted the brink of Sanderson Canyon, one wall of which rose over the main street of the town.

Shadow, his magnificent black horse, looked pensive and was perhaps indulging in similar cogitations, although probably the prospect of a succulent helping of oats in the near future was uppermost in his mind. He began negotiating the downward slope, the murmur and grumble of Sanderson's activities steadily loudening from the depths.

'Well, feller, so far we have enjoyed

peace and quiet all the way from Browns-ville,' Slade remarked. 'But I've a hunch it won't last. Sheriff Tom Crane doesn't write Captain Jim asking for help with-out ample reason for doing so.'

The Captain Jim in question was Captain James McNelty, the famed Commander of the Border Battalion of the Texas Rangers.

'No, old Tom doesn't cut loose a squawk just to beat his gums together,' Slade added. 'So let's go and see what's what.'

Slade made a picture once seen never forgotten as he lounged gracefully atop his great black horse. Very tall, more than six feet, the breadth of his shoulders and the depth of his chest that slimmed down to a lean, sinewy waist were in keeping with his splendid height.

His face was as arresting as his form, A rather wide mouth, grin-quirked at the corners, somewhat relieved the tinge of fierceness evinced by the prominent hawk nose above and the powerful jaw and chin beneath. His pushed-back J. B.

revealed a broad forehead and crisp, thick hair as black as Shadow's midnight coat.

The sternly handsome countenance was dominated by long, black-lashed eyes of very pale gray, the color of a glacier lake under a stormy sky. Cold, reckless eyes that nevertheless always seemed to have gay little devils of laughter dancing in their clear depths. Devils that could, did occasion warrant, leap to the front and be anything but laughing. Then those eyes were 'the terrible eyes of *El Halcón*,' before whose bleak stare armed and plenty salty gents had been known to quail and back down in a hurry.

Slade wore the efficient garb of the rangeland, and lent dignity to the homely dress-Levis, the bibless overalls favored by the cowhands, soft blue shirt with vivid neckerchief looped at the throat, well-scuffed halfboots of softly tanned leather, and the broad-brimmed hat, the rainshed of the plains.

Around his waist were double cartridge belts, from the carefully worked and oiled cut-out holsters of which protruded the plain black butts of heavy guns. And from the butts of those big Colt forty-fives, his slender, muscular hands seemed never far away.

Snugged in his saddle boot was a long-range Winchester rifle, a 'special' procured for him by his old *amigo* James G. 'Jaggers' Dunn, the famed General Manager of the great C. & P. Railroad system, who had a habit of getting whatever he went after, be it a corporation or a rifle.

Now he was nearing the bottom of the sag and the confused chorus of sounds were separating like drops of water on a tautly strung wire. The scream of whistles, the booming of locomotive exhausts, the clang-jangle of brake riggings, the hum of machine shops, and the babble of voices.

Slade's pulses quickened. He liked Sanderson, which was always gay and colorful.

His first stop was at a stable that had serviced Shadow before, and where he knew the big black would get the best of attention.

The stable keeper, an elderly and competent Mexican, had a warm greeting for both man and horse, plus a low bow to *El Halcón*. Having formerly been introduced to the one-man horse who permitted nobody to put a hand on him without his master's sanction, he stroked Shadow's glossy neck, the big black accepting the familiarity in a bored fashion, with a glance at his feed box.

'Shine he will when next you see him, *Capitán*,' the keeper assured Slade.

'I know he will, Manuel, he's in good hands,' Slade replied. The old Mexican beamed.

The sun had set in polychromatic glory when Slade left the stable and turned his steps to the sheriff's office. Soon it would be night.

When he entered the office, grizzled, lanky old Sherill Tom Crane leaped to his feet, hand outstretched.

'Blazes! This is fine, plumb fine!' he exclaimed. 'Didn't expect you to get here so soon.'

'I was in Brownsville when I got Captain Jim's word,' Slade explained. 'Isn't such a far ride.'

'Not forking Shadow,' the sheriff agreed. 'Squat, and I'll get us some coffee from the back room; pot simmerin'.'

The coffee was soon forthcoming. Slade glanced expectantly over the rim of his cup.

'Well, what's the trouble, Tom?' he asked.

'Plenty,' growled the sheriff. 'Remember, a while back the Big Bend outlaws kinda tried to move into town but were squelched, largely by you. Well, now they *have* moved in and are operating here. Three rumholes held up, bartender knifed. Four stores robbed or burgled, clerk murdered, another knife killing. More cow critters to the west, north, and east widelooped than for a long time. As you know, we've always been bothered by that, but not like of late. Stagecoach robbed, driver shot to pieces from the brush. Oh, there's hell aplenty busted loose.'

'Any notion as to who is responsible?'

That's the trouble,' replied Crane. 'The hellions are just like shadows. Seem to come from nowhere, make a strike, and vanish into nowhere. Figure they roust have a hole-up here in town, but don't know about that for sure.'

'Has a familiar ring,' Slade commented. 'Crater Morales and his bunch were like that, but they were finally rooted out.'

'Again mostly your doings,' said the sheriff. 'That's why I sent for you — nobody else has had any luck against them. Got a notion things will be sorta different now.'

'Hope you are right,' Slade smiled. 'I'll do the best I can.'

'Which will be puhlenty!' predicted Crane.

'How about the little oil-strike town down to the southeast? Tumble, I believe they call it.'

'That hell-hole!' snorted the sheriff. 'All the owlhoots that haven't congregated in Sanderson hang out there. I spend more time there than here.'

'Don't let it worry you,' Slade counseled. 'That's always the way with a strike town, whether it's gold, silver, oil or what have you. But it won't last. That shallow pool will soon be pumped out, the town will disintegrate, and, as I have said relative to other such fly-by-night *pueblos*, another generation won't believe it ever existed.'

'Maybe not, but I'm of this generation and it's breathing down my neck,' grunted Crane. 'And that spur Jaggers Dunn ran up from the east-west railroad hasn't improved matters — makes it easier for the blasted wind spiders to reach Tumble.'

'I believe you mentioned that you've had a lot of cow stealing,' Slade observed.

'That's right, plenty,' replied the sheriff, 'From all the spreads.'

'Cows provide a quick money turnover,' Slade remarked thoughtfully. 'But wideloopers are vulnerable, and may provide us with opportunity, as they have done before. I'd like to have the line-up of the spreads to the east of Tumble.'

The sheriff pondered a moment. 'Well,' he said, 'first is Bob Kerr's Four K. Then comes Martin Gladden's Lazy G. Next is Fisher Farrow's Double F. Then Ed Duval's Rocking D, that laps over into Valverde County. Up to the north is Redman Widgen's Square W., which is long east by west, narrow north by south.'

'As I recall them,' Slade remarked. 'And all except Widgen's holding running to the Rio Grande on the south.'

'Guess that's right,' Crane conceded.

'I'm fairly conversant with the section but never bothered to get the names of the owners. And they've all lost cows?'

'Right again,' said Crane, 'I — what in hell!'

2

The building shook to a muffled explosion not far off. It was almost immediately followed by a crackle of gunfire and a wild yelling. Slade and the sheriff leaped to their feet and rushed to the door.

There was nobody in sight, but the shooting and yelling were swiftly drawing nearer.

Around the near corner bulged four horseman going like the wind, A yelp of alarm, the blaze of a gun, and a slug fanned Slade's face.

El Halcón did not take kindly to being shot at by perfect strangers. He registered his disapproval by whipping out his big Colts and letting drive.

A gurgling, retching cry echoed the boom of the forty-fives, One of the riders flopped to the ground, writhed an instant, stiffened out.

Answering bullets buzzed around the weaving, shifting Ranger like angry hornets. One barely touched his left temple the shock throwing him a trifle off balance, and he scored a miss.

But not the next time he squeezed trigger. A second man reeled sideways and fell, to lie motionless. The two remaining swerved around the far corner, Slade pouring lead after them, and kept going. Thumbs hooked over the hammers of his guns, Slade's eyes never left the forms on the ground.

'Take it easy,' he told the storming sheriff. 'I think they are both dead, and the other two escaped. Are you all right?'

'Never touched met replied Crane. 'How could they with you keeping in front of me all the time?'

Around the near corner streamed a yelling, cursing crowd. 'Did you get 'em, Sheriff?' somebody bawled. 'Slade got two of them, the other two made it in the clear,' the sheriff shouted reply. 'Shut up your jabberin' and tell us what it's all about.'

The hullabaloo lessened a trifle. A voice cut through it: 'The blankety-blanks robbed Bunty's store, knocked out the watchman or shot him or something. Feller who happened to look through the window right after the dynamite or something exploded saw the watchman layin' on the floor and the devils taking a money poke outa the safe. He started running and yelling. Out they came, forked horses standing at a rack, and hightailed, shooting in every direction.'

'All right, some of you pack the carcasses into the office and lay 'em on the floor,' Crane ordered.

'Then everybody out and lock the door, Tom,' Slade added. 'I want a look at the watchman. Somebody hurry and fetch Doc Cooper. And catch those two horses and bring them here.'

The horses, well trained and docile beasts, had run but a few yards and were easily caught. Slade went through the saddle pouches and, with an exclamation of satisfaction, drew forth from the second a plumb rawhide poke. Loosening the pucker string revealed packets of bills and rolls of gold coin.

'The luck broke for us,' he observed

to Crane. 'Managed to down the one packing the money.'

'Well, I'll be hanged, that is luck!' sputtered the sheriff. 'The luck of *El Halcón* — never fails.'

'You're too optimistic,' Slade smiled. 'Take the cayuses to Manuel's stable, fellows, and tell him *El Halcón* said to take care of them.'

'*El Halcón*!' somebody muttered. 'By gosh, it is Mr. Slade, the sheriff's special deputy.'

One and all the crowd, constantly augmented by new arrivals, gazed almost in awe at the man whose exploits, some of them thought questionable in certain quarters, were fast becoming legendary throughout the Southwest and elsewhere.

'Come on, Tom,' Slade said, 'I want to have a look at the watchman as quickly as possible; can't help but be a bit worried about him. I figure the devils as a killer bunch.'

However, his fears were somewhat relieved when they reached the store office. The watchman had recovered consciousness and was sitting in a chair, holding his bloody head in his hands.

A quick examination revealed no bone fracture so far as Slade could ascertain, and he believed there was no evidence of concussion.

'Caught him a slanting blow with a gun barrel and just temporarily stunned him,' the Ranger said to Crane. 'Wouldn't be surprised if they thought they had killed him, which quite probably they intended to do.'

'Here comes Doc Cooper!' somebody shouted.

'Well, how is it?' the old frontier practitioner asked Slade after they shook hands.

'I'd say he isn't badly hurt,' *El Halcón* replied.

'If you say he isn't, he isn't,' Cooper declared. 'Those hands of yours are never wrong. A mighty fine surgeon was lost when you decided to be — something else. I'll patch him up a bit and administer a stimulant, and then you can talk with him if you wish.'

While the doctor was working on his patient, Slade looked the room over. The windows were shattered by the explosion. The safe door lay in front of the safe. Slade shook his head.

'The work of experts,' he told Crane. 'Drilled a hole in the face of the safe, poured in the soup — nitroglycerin — between the door casings and set it off with a short fuse and a percussion cap. You'll notice the door was little more than knocked off the hinges. Perfect timing, and perfect measuring of the explosive. Yes, the work of experts. Tom, I'm afraid we are up against something out of the ordinary.'

'With *El Halcón* on the job, I ain't worried,' was the cheerful rejoinder. Slade laughed and turned to the watchman, who was puffing on a cigarette and looking much improved.

However, he could tell Slade little. 'Was just getting ready to lay out my lunch when I heard something behind me,' he said. 'Started to turn around and

16

got just a glimpse of a big, tall hellion loomin' over me. Next thing, the sky fell in.'

'Didn't get a look at his face?'

The watchman shook his head. 'Hardly more than a glimmer,' he replied. 'Sorta seemed he had whiskers, but I ain't even sure about that.'

'Guess you might as well have him packed to your office, if you're of a mind to, Doc,' Slade suggested to Cooper.

'I'll do that,' the doctor replied. 'Some of you fellers hustle to my place and fetch the stretcher you'll find there — door isn't locked. I'll keep an eye on the old coot overnight.'

Several men hurried to care for the chore. Somebody exclaimed, 'Here comes Bunty!'

The owner entered quickly, concern written on his pleasant, elderly face. His first concern was for the watchman, and he expressed relief upon learning he was not seriously injured.

'By the way, wasn't the outside door supposed to be locked?' Slade asked the

17

watchman.

'I know darn well I locked it when I came in from making my rounds,' the watchman insisted.

Slade crossed to the door and found the key was in the lock, on the inside of the door. He drew it forth, held it to the light, and studied it a moment.

'Thought so,' he said. 'See the tiny abrasions on the metal, Tom?'

'I can't see anything,' growled the sheriff. 'Those eyes of yours!'

'Slipped a pair of thin-jawed pliers into the keyhole from the outside, gripped the key and turned it to shoot the bolt,' Slade explained. 'Easy enough for somebody knowing how, and evidently our *amigos* know how.'

Bunty shook his head in wordless admiration.

'And by the way again, here's your money poke, Bunty,' the sheriff said, slipping it from under his coat.

'W-w-what!' stuttered the astonished owner.

'Slade managed to down the homed

toad who was packing the *dinero*,' Crane chuckled. 'Figured you could use it.'

'I sure can,' sighed Bunty. 'Part payment for a new building I plan to put up. This is sure mighty fine.' He glanced at Slade, took several big bills from a packet, glanced again at the smiling Ranger, dropped the bills back in the poke and said simply, 'Thank you, Mr. Slade.'

The sheriff glanced around, tugged his mustache.

'Looks like everything is under control here,' he remarked. 'How about Hardrock Hogan's and a couple of snorts and a bite?'

'I can go for a bite,' Slade replied. 'Haven't had anything since before dawn. Let's go! Goodnight, everybody.'

Hardrock Hogan was a former miner and prospector who had made a small strike, invested the proceedings in the Branding Pen saloon and restaurant, and made a big strike, the Branding Pen being a money maker from the start.

Hardrock was big and burly, with an

underslung jaw, a wide, almost reptilian mouth, a crooked nose, bristling red hair, and narrowed eyes of the palest green. Not exactly a prepossessing individual at first glance. But he was a squareshooter and ran his place strictly on the up-and-up. Nobody need fear of being misused in the Branding Pen, and if he had only a couple of pesos to spend, he was made as welcome as another with a well-filled poke. Hardrock picked his drink jugglers, dealers, waiters, and floormen with care. He demanded loyalty and good behavior, and got it. Very seldom was there trouble in the Branding Pen, and did a rukus start, Hardrock usually handled the situation without help.

He gave a joyous bellow and came plowing across the room to greet Slade.

'How are you, Mr. Slade?' he chuckled. 'Hear you've already begun mopping up the hellions. A little more and we'll have peace and quiet hereabouts for a change. The sidewinders are going to find out what it means to go up against *El Halcón*.

Come along, come along! Got your favorite table reserved for you, close to the dance floor so the gals can get a good look at a real gent.'

'Thank you, Hardrock,' Slade smiled reply. 'I appreciate your solicitude, and I guess the girls can put up with it.'

The dance-floor girls were young and pretty, but Slade knew that shrewd old Hardrock also realized that from that particular table he had a clear view of the windows, the swinging doors, and most of the room as reflected in the back-bar mirror.

3

The Branding Pen was big, brightly lighted, excellently appointed, and spotlessly clean from its long, shining bar to its commodious dance floor, both of which were doing a rousing business. There was a lunch counter, tables for leisurely eaters, two roulette wheels spinning merrily, and a faro bank.

'My Mexican cook and his helpers know *El Halcón* is here and are doing their damndest,' said Hardrock. 'They feel it is a great honor to serve him; you'll get the best the house has to offer, and on the house, of course. Gotta keep on the right side of the Law or get closed up.'

'Should be on general principles,' grunted the sheriff. 'All rumholes are a nuisance.' Hardrock chuckled.

Slade's entrance was the signal for whoops of greeting and praise, but Hardrock shooed everybody away so Ranger and sheriff could enjoy their meal in peace. It took a little time to prepare, but when it arrived it was well worth waiting for, and both proceeded to do it full justice.

After they finished eating, Slade repaired to the kitchen to thank the cook and his helpers for the really excellent repast. All bowed low to *El Halcón*.

The helpers were lithe young Yaqui-Mexicans of a type that had rendered him help more than once in the past. He chatted with them for a while in his flawless Spanish and left them happy.

For some time Slade and the sheriff sat smoking and sipping; the sheriff a helpin' of redeye, Slade coffee.

Slade listened to scraps of conversation his keen ears caught, studied faces. Finally the sheriff remarked, 'Lots of newcomers since you were here last. Some not so good, some all right. A couple of distinguished gents at the bar right now who 'pear to be up and coming. The big tall feller talking to Hardrock is one. Name's Clag,

Bertram Clag. He's a representative of an oil company over east, around the Spindletop field at Beaumont. Spends a good deal of his time at Tumble. The other one, the tall jigger about midway along the bar is Haley Welch. He bought Charley Dawson's carting business. You remember Charley, of course. Welch went to Mary Merril, who owns a couple of trains, and asked her if she minded competition. She told him to go right ahead, there was plenty of business for another train. Wanted to give him a break, of course; she's made that way. Welch started servicing the gold, silver, copper, lead, quicksilver, and zinc mines over between Marathon and Alpine, something nobody else had ever thought of, and is doing all right by himself. Services some of the big spreads, too. Makes a run now and then down to the Terlingua quicksilver mines in the Big Bend. Yep, he's okay.'

Slade regarded both Welch and Clag with interest. Both were big men, both straight-featured with firm mouths and deep-set eyes pale blue or gray in coloring. Both, he thought, were on the handsome side in a rugged, big-featured way. The only marked difference he could note was in the hair, Clag's being rather light brown, Welch's black as Slade's own. Yes, rather distinguished appearing men and no doubt capable. He dismissed them from his thoughts for the time being.

'Mary Merril still has her carting business?' he asked casually, giving the sheriff an opening.

'Sure,' he replied. 'And she's going strong. She services Tumble, of course, has Westbrook Lerner's contract tied up tight. Lerner who, as you know, brought in the first Tumble well and runs the field, swears by her. Says he never had such service, Her other train makes the run to Gato, the silver town down to the southwest at the edge of the Big Bend country. She's a darn good businesswoman, smart as she's pretty. Owns half of her uncle John Webb's big spread, that he deeded her as a twenty-first birthday gift. She's well heeled. Betcha she'll be showing up pronto when she learns you're here.'

'I hope so,' Slade said. 'She's all right. Well, I'm going to pick up my saddle pouches at the stable and register for a room at the Regan House and call it a night. Has been a long and busy day. We'll look over the bodies tomorrow. Suppose Doc Cooper, as coroner, will want to hold an inquest.'

'Oh, sure,' answered Crane. 'No hurry; they'll keep, and they ain't going anywhere. See you tomorrow.' Slade sauntered out, admiring glances following his progress to the swinging doors.

'Same old story, Shadow,' he said, bestowing a pat before leaving the stable. 'Already developing a familiar pattern. That store robbery tonight has been duplicated a score of times, here and elsewhere, during the past couple of years. Seems people can never learn not to leave money in those old cast-iron boxes that can almost be opened with a screwdriver. Oh, well, business as usual for us. Expect we'll make out. See you tomorrow, horse.'

He walked to the door, his pouches hooked over his shoulder, flipped it open, stepping back a little, as was his habit when opening a door.

As the door swung wide, he went sideways in a catlike leap as he sensed movement in the shadows on the far side of the alley.

A gun blazed, the slug whizzing past in front of him. Weaving, ducking, he flickered his Colts from their sheaths and shot with both hands, again, and again.

There was a coughing groan, a man lurched from the shadows and sprawled forward on his face. Still doing his slithering dance, Slade probed the shadows, his all-embracing glance including the motionless form on the ground.

Nothing more happened; evidently the drygulcher had been alone, and the one on the ground was undoubtedly done for, drilled dead center.

Manuel, the keeper, was storming down the stairs, swearing in three languages and waving wildly a double-barreled sawed-off six-gauge shotgun, the enormous muzzles looking like blackened nail kegs.

'Hold it!' Slade told him. 'Everything under control. And put down the hammers on that old baseburner. If it cuts loose it'll blow Sanderson into the Rio Grande.'

'You all right are, *Capitán*?' Manuel asked anxiously, obeying orders and uncocking the shotgun. 'Fine as frog hair,' Slade replied.

'But what was it, *Capitán*, why you shoot?'

'Just a little try at a drygulching that didn't work,' Slade answered cheerfully as he began rolling a cigarette with the slim fingers of his left hand, having already replaced the spent shells in his guns with fresh cartridges. He gestured to the body on the ground, Manuel said things in English, Spanish, and Yaqui, and peered at the still form.

'What deserved he got did he,' he said. 'Somebody comes!'

In fact, quite a few somebodies were coming, most of the Branding Pen patrons, the stable being quite close to the saloon. Others were backing them up, and leading the pack was Sheriff Tom Crane, outdoing Manuel in profanity.

'I knew it!' he bawled. 'Soon as I heard a gun crack I knew you were mixed in something. I see you plugged a hellion. A little try at getting rid of you, eh?'

'Looks a little that way,' Slade conceded. 'Didn't work, and that's all that matters.'

'Ho! Ho! Ho!' bellowed somebody with the lungs of a stentor. 'Figured to get the drop on *El Halcón*! Might as well go chasin' after moonbeams, or try to light a candle from a star, as the saying goes. Keep up the good work, Mr. Slade, we're for you!'

'Thank you,' Slade acknowledged. 'I'm liable to need all the help I can get.'

'I doubt it,' boomed Stentor. 'Figure you'll handle by yourself anything that turns up.'

'And now suppose everybody stow their gabbin' for a while and pack the carcass to my office,' said the sheriff. Willing volunteers at once stepped forward.

Slade held them up long enough to give the body a quick once-over. A hard-lined face with nothing outstanding about it, so far as he could ascertain.

'Will give it a more thorough examination tomorrow,' he said to Crane. 'Yes, he was holed up in the shadows on the far side of the alley. Made the mistake of shifting position a trifle before he lined sights.'

'A darn bad mistake on his part,' grunted the sheriff. 'And now I'm going to make another try at the Regan House and a room,' Slade said. 'See you tomorrow.'

He bestowed another pat on Shadow, spoke soothingly to the other nervous horses, said goodnight to Manuel and made it to the Regan House without further misadventure. Registering for a room, he tumbled into bed and was almost instantly asleep.

The midmorning sun was peeping through chinks in the blind when Slade awoke, thoroughly rested and in a complacent frame of mind. He bathed, shaved, donned a clean shirt and overalls and prepared to sally forth in search of breakfast.

As he stepped out the door, the one to the room next to his opened and a touseled head of dark curls appeared.

4

She wore a blue robe that enhanced the color of her big eyes and certainly did nothing to detract from the luscious curves of her small form. She skipped out and was in his arms!

'One kiss, and then sift sand away from here before somebody comes along and starts a scandal,' Miss Mary Merril giggled as he snugged her close. 'I'll have breakfast with you at the Branding Pen.'

Slade obeyed orders and was shortly sitting at his table, waiting.

He didn't have long to wait. Very quickly she appeared, modishly attired.

'Very lovely, but not more so than your blue shirt and overalls,' Slade commented approvingly.

'A girl has to dress up now and then, or everybody will forget she's feminine,' Mary retorted.

'Not everybody,' he differed with a heartiness that caused the roses to bloom in her creamily tanned cheeks.

'How'd you know I was in town?' he asked.

'I didn't, till I saw your name on the register,' she replied. 'I came right to the hotel, shortly after midnight, being dog tired, when we rolled in from Tumble. We had cart trouble on the way and were held up for quite a while to make repairs. A singular coincidence, was it not, that we should have adjoining rooms?'

'The desk clerk is an *amigo* of mine,' Slade replied, obliquely.

'Mine, too,' Mary smiled. 'Now tell me what you've been into since you landed here. No, don't. Here comes the sheriff and he'll give me the real lowdown, which you won't. Hello, Uncle Tom, tell me what he's been mixed up in.'

The sheriff obliged vividly and in detail. Mary sighed and shook her curly head.

'Never a moment of peace!' she lamented. 'Always something to get me disturbed about.'

'Don't worry about him,' Crane

advised. 'I don't.'

'You do, but you won't admit it,' Mary retorted. 'Besides, you're not a woman.'

'So I've always been given to understand,' the sheriff corroborated.

'Well, here comes breakfast; that should keep her quiet for a while,' Slade remarked.

'So I talk too much, do I? I'll make you talk before I've finished with you.'

'And that I don't doubt,' chuckled Crane. 'A man will always talk between — '

'And that will be enough from you,' Mary interrupted. 'Let's eat!' They did.

The comparative peace and quiet of the Branding Pen was shattered by a roaring entrance. The carters had finished their chores and were ready to celebrate.

'Hi, Mr. Slade!' was the bellowed chorus. 'How you been? Gotta have a couple on us. Fill 'em up, waiter!'

The carters wished a drink served him from each of their number, but Slade insisted a couple on the bunch would be sufficient.

'Let them have their way and I'd have to be rolled out,' he said, raising his glass in salute.

The sheriff and Mary also came in for a helpin' on the bunch, the sheriff risking two, Mary compromising on a small glass of wine.

After which the carters' interest turned to their drinks the cards, and the dance-floor girls. Which was as it should be.

'Doc Cooper would like to hold an inquest on those three carcasses in an hour or so,' Crane remarked. 'He has a patient to visit in the afternoon and wants to get the chore off his hands. Darn foolishness, of course, but reeks on he figures he has to do something to earn his pay as coroner.'

'All right with me,' Slade replied.

'I went through their pockets but didn't lie onto anything that counts, so far as I could see,' the sheriff continued. 'That is except quite a passel of money, which wasn't surprising for, as I told you, the hellions have been doing pretty good for themselves. I put the junk in my desk drawer so you can look it over if you are a mind to.'

'Anybody remember seeing them before?'

'Oh, some barkeeps felt sure they'd served 'em at one time or another but couldn't remember anything about them. Same old story there. Seems they always behaved and didn't attract attention to themselves.'

'As was to be expected,' Slade said. 'I presume the head of the bunch keeps a pretty light rein on his followers and won't stand for any shenanigans in town.'

'Chances are you're right,' Crane agreed.

'And I've got to hurry to the station this minute and check loads with Mr. Lerner,' Mary said. 'He planned to ride in this morning and should be here now, waiting for me. I'll have dinner with you tonight and we'll do the town. That is, if you don't go gallivanting off somewhere.'

'I certainly don't expect to,' Slade assured her. She trotted out, Bashing a smile over her shoulder, her little even teeth startlingly white against the scarlet of her lips.

'That walk of hers would make a bull-dog break his chain,' sighed the sheriff. 'Oh, to be fifty again!'

A few minutes later the sheriff and Slade also departed, to the accompaniment of more whoops from the carters, who were well on the way to getting organized.

The inquest was held, with the jury's verdict no surprise to anybody. The deceased met their deaths at the hand of a law-enforcement officer in the performance of his duty. Slade was complimented on a good chore, the hope expressed that there would be a repeat performance in the near future.

Before the undertaker packed the bodies to Boot Hill, Slade carefully examined the dead hands.

'The one that tried to drygulch me in the alley was a cowhand a long time ago,' he told the sheriff. 'Marks of rope and branding iron still discernible, although faint. The other two who took part in the

Bunty store robbery never were. Which is not surprising. As I mentioned, that showed the handiwork of experts, certainly not former range riders.'

'Then what the devil were they?' Crane wondered.

'Hard to tell,' Slade replied. 'River pirates, perhaps, or worked on railroads, or in the oil fields, or on big city jobs. Smarter, more widely experienced, often with better education than the oldtimers. Utterly ruthless, putting no greater value on a man's life than on that of a fly. One redeeming virtue of the oldtimers was that they seldom killed wantonly. The new brand we are getting is different. And unfortunately, from our viewpoint, with more brains, and the know-how to use them.'

'Uh-huh, but I don't forget what Captain McNelty says of you,' said the sheriff. 'That you not only outshoot the sidewinders, you outthink 'em, too. So I ain't overly bothered; my money's still on *El Halcón*.'

'Hope your confidence isn't misplaced,' Slade smiled.

'It ain't,' the sheriff declared positively.

Slade glanced at the rubhish the sheriff had drawn from the outlaws' pockets and discovered nothing he considered of importance until he came to a folded slip of paper on which were lines, numbers, and symbols.

'What is it?' the sheriff asked, peering over his shoulder.

'It is a very neatly drawn plat of a trail,' Slade replied. 'May mean nothing, but then again it could be important Somehow the terrain depicted strikes a chord of memory in my mind, although just where or what I have no idea at the moment. It's a plat, all right, drawn by an engineering or surveying hand.'

'Well, if the best engineer that ever rode across Texas says it is, I guess it is,' said Crane. Slade laughed and did not comment.

However, the sheriff was not too far off, as Jaggers Dunn, former Texas Governor and oil millionaire Jim Hogg, John Warne 'Bet a Million' Gates, the Wall Street tycoon, and others of similar ilk would have maintained.

Shortly before the death of his father, which occurred after financial reverses that entailed the loss of the elder Slade's ranch, young Walt had graduated with high honors from a noted college of engineering. He had planned to take a post-graduate course in certain subjects to round out his education and better lit him for the profession he had resolved to make his life work.

But that became economically impossible at the moment, and Slade was sort of at loose ends and undecided which way to turn when Captain Jim McNelty, with whom Slade had worked some during summer vacations, suggested he sign up with the Rangers for a while and pursue his studies in spare time. Slade quickly concluded the suggestion a good one.

So Walt Slade became a Texas Ranger. Long since he had gotten more from private study than he could have hoped for from the post-grad and was eminently fitted for the profession of engineering.

But meanwhile Ranger work had gotten a strong hold on him, providing as it did so many opportunities for doing good, combating evil, helping the deserving, and making Texas, and America, a better land for the right kind of people. And as the years flowed past, he still repeated to himself that he was young, plenty of time to be an engineer, although he had already received tempting offers of lucrative employment from such figures as Dunn, Hogg, and Gates. Yes, plenty of time to be an engineer; he'd stick with the Rangers a while longer.

Which was quite probably what shrewd old Captain Jim expected when he offered the suggestion.

Due to his habit of working alone as much as possible, and often undercover, Slade had built up a singular dual reputation. Those who, like Sheriff Tom Crane, knew the truth insisted that he was not only the most fearless but also the ablest of the Rangers, while others who knew him only as *El Halcón* with killings to his credit, maintained that he was just an owlhoot himself, able to pull the wool over the eyes of gullible sheriffs and too smart to get caught, so far.

Among these latter, however, Slade had staunch supporters who pointed out that he always worked on the side of law and order and that anybody he killed had a killing coming and over-due.

The deception worried Captain McNelty, who feared his Lieutenant and undercover ace-man might come to harm because of it. But he gave in when Slade pointed out that as *El Halcón* he was able to open avenues of information that would be closed to a known Ranger, and that outlaws, thinking him one of their own brand, sometimes got careless, to their grief.

So Slade blithely went his way as *El Halcón*, satisfied with the present and bothering about the future none at all. And treasuring most what was said by the Mexican *peónes* and other humble folk:

'*El Halcón*! The good! The just! The compassionate! The friend of the lowly! May *El Dias* ever guard him!'

5

'Now what?' the sheriff asked, surveying the floor minus carcasses with disapproval.

Slade glanced out the window. 'It's getting dark, so I'm heading for the Branding Pen to meet Mary,' he replied. 'Told her I would.'

'Okay,' nodded Crane. 'I'll meet you there in a little while; got some work to do. Watch your step.'

When Slade reached the Branding Pen, Mary Merril wasn't there.

'She went over to the hotel to freshen up a bit, she said,' Hardrock reported. 'Finished her loads. Mr. Lerner is still at the station, tallying the money he brought from Tumble against the loads. He buys for the whole field.'

'Did she say he was there alone?' Slade asked.

'Why, I guess he is,' answered Hardrock. 'All the carters and outriders are at the bar or on the dance floor. Yes, he must be.'

'Will they *ever* learn!' Slade exclaimed, and was out the door before the bewildered Hardrock could open his mouth.

Hoping against hope that he'd be in time, Slade raced for the cart station, which sat at the lower end of town, flanked by a small grove and a bristle of chaparral. As he drew near, he saw that a light burned in the office. He had almost reached the station when the light abruptly snapped out. Another moment and Lerner loomed in the door, packing a plump poke under his arm.

And from the growth glided three men, guns trained on the driller. Slade's voice rang out:

'Up! You are under arrest!'

With startled exclamations, the trio whirled to face him, guns jutting forward. Both Slade's Colts blazed.

Down went one man, writhing and twitching, slamming into one of his companions as he went down, throwing him off balance. The third lined sights with the Ranger's breast.

But the money poke, hurled by Lerner, caught him squarely in the face, and the slug intended for his heart merely fanned Slade's face. *El Halcón's* Colts finished him. The remaining outlaw dashed into the brush and out of sight, his speeding feet thudding into the distance.

Slade didn't dare follow him; the pair on the ground were still moving slightly.

'Hold it, stay where you are!' he snapped at Lerner, his eyes never leaving the forms sprawled in the dust. But quickly their movements ceased and they lay supine. Slade reloaded his guns and proceeded to give the oil man a good dressing down.

'I thought you would have better sense than to be alone here, packing all that money,' he concluded.

'I guess I made a mistake,' Lerner admitted shame-facedly. 'One of the boys was here when Mary left, but I told him to go on and join the fun, that I wouldn't need him.'

'You did need him,' Slade replied.

'And it's just pure luck that your mistake wasn't fatal.'

'Luck, plus some mighty straight shooting on your part,' returned Lerner.

'That money poke you threw helped,' Slade said, somewhat mollified by the way Lerner took his scolding. 'Looked like I might collect an airhole in my hide.'

'I doubt it,' replied Lerner, 'but nice to think I may have been of help. I'm sure plenty deep in your debt. Wasn't for you, I reckon I'd be dead now.' Slade did not argue the point, being of the same opinion.

Shouts were sounding in the distance, quickly drawing nearer. The shots had been heard, of course, and people were coming to investigate. Soon they were the center of a chattering crowd that grew by the minute.

'Shut up your gabbling!' Slade thundered, getting something like silence. 'Somebody fetch the sheriff.'

'Please tell us what happened, Mr. Slade,' a voice called above the general turmoil.

Lerner told them, graphically.

'Always Johnny-on-the-Spot when he's needed, that's Mr. Slade,' somebody chuckled. There was a chorus of agreement.

The sheriff soon put in an appearance, close behind him Hardrock Hogan, Deputy Ester, and Mary Merril. The story was repeated for their benefit.

'I'm partly to blame myself; I should have stayed with him until the money tally was completed,' Mary said.

'I'm glad you didn't,' Slade told her. 'Flying lead plays no favorites.'

'I've dodged flying lead before now,' was the composed answer, which was so.

'All right, some of you worthless coots pack the carcasses to my office and lay 'em on the floor,' ordered Crane. 'More work for Doc Cooper.'

'And for the jiggers whose chore is to plant 'em,' was a cheerful addition.

'Go along with 'em, Ester,' Crane directed the deputy. 'We'll look 'em over later. Right now I hanker for some snorts and a bite to eat. Come on, Walt; bring

Mary and Lerner with you. Guess you've got your money poke stowed away, eh, Lerner?'

'I sure have, right here under my arm, thanks to Mr. Slade, Plenty in it, too,' Lerner replied.

When they reached the Branding Pen, Lerner, who had eaten his lunch late in the afternoon, at once joined the carters at the bar and was soon the center of attraction as he recounted the details of the robbery attempt. Hands were waved to Slade, greetings and praise whooped.

Slade gazed affectionately at the slender little man with his leathery, poreless-looking skin and bright eyes.

'Would have grieved me had something bad happened to him,' he remarked. 'A fine, generous man, always ready to lend a helping hand. When he bought in the Tumble field, he at once threw the field wide open to anybody desiring to put down a well; he does things like that all the time. Owns a number of wells at the great Spindletop field, but he's a true wildcatter. Never happier than when opening up a new field. He won't stay here long. Soon he'll be off on the prowl for another strike. Make one and he'll give it away.'

'Those wildcat drillers are just the same as chuck-line-riding cowhands,' grunted the sheriff. 'Always on the move.'

'Like others of the same brand,' Mary said with a sigh.

They took their time at dinner, and the evening was wearing along when they had finished eating.

'And now I guess we'd better amble to the office and give the carcasses a once-over,' the sheriff said to Slade as he stuffed tobacco into his pipe.

'And when you get back, I want to dance and to do the town, so please try and keep out of trouble,' Mary requested.

'Do the best we can,' Crane promised cheerfully. 'Let's go, Walt.'

When they reached the office, they found only a few loiterers keeping the deputy company. These Crane shooed out. He drew the blind and locked the door.

'Yes, four or five people, including a couple of barkeeps, were sure they'd seen the horned toads in town, but didn't remember anything much about them,' Ester replied to a question from the sheriff.

'Important only that it tends to confirm my belief that the bunch hangs out in Sanderson, for the most part at least,' Slade observed as he examined the dead hands.

'These were never cowhands,' he reported. 'Looks like range riders are in the minority, which is not comforting, indicating as it does that we have more and better brains to contend with than we usually have.'

'You'll contend with 'em,' predicted Crane. 'The devils are going to find what it means to contend with real brains, *El Halcón* brains.'

'Your confidence is inspiring,' Slade said smilingly.

The outlaw pockets revealed nothing of significance, so far as Slade could judge, except quite a bit of money, although not so much as the former specimens produced.

'Wouldn't be surprised if losing out on a couple of good hauls will sorta hurt the hellions,' said the sheriff.

'Which means we can look for more trouble soon,' Slade answered. 'The head of the bunch must keep his followers supplied with plenty of spending money if he hopes to keep them in line, so he'll be making a try at something very quickly. The big questions for us being When and Where.'

As he spoke, he drew from his pocket the plat of a trail he had taken off the body of the dead store-robber and studied it, the concentration furrow deep between his black brows a sure sign *El Halcón* was doing some hard thinking.

'The meaning of this thing continues to elude me,' he said slowly. 'But I have a growing conviction that it is important. I can almost vision the terrain over which the trail runs, but not quite.'

'It will come to you, sooner or later,' the sheriff predicted.

'Hope it doesn't come too late to do us good,' Slade replied.

'It won't,' insisted Crane, still optimistic. 'Well, reckon we'd better shut up shop and head for the Branding Pen before your gal has a conniption duck fit and comes looking for us. You might as well call it a night, too, Ester. Let's go.'

The lights were doused, the door locked, and they departed, Slade and the sheriff to the Branding Pen, Ester for parts unknown.

They found Mary chatting with Lerner and not too perturbed. Nor Was Lerner.

'Money poke locked up in Hardrock's safe,' he said. 'Ain't got a care in the world.'

'You don't need to have any where the money is concerned,' Slade replied. 'His safe is a good and new one, and only somebody utterly loco would try to hold up or burgle the Branding Pen. Not with the kind of floormen, waiters, and bartenders he's got, to say nothing of those Yaqui knife men in the kitchen. Money's safe.'

'That's the way I feel about it,' nodded Lerner. 'And into the bank it goes in the morning as soon as the bank's open, with four or five of the boys convoying me. I done learned my lesson, Mr. Slade.'

'A pity I can't learn one where he's concerned,' sighed Mary. 'Then maybe I wouldn't be afflicted by the jitters half the time.'

'Yes, but look at the fun you'd miss,' the sheriff pointed out. Mary did not look altogether impressed. That is, until her eyes met Slade's laughing regard and she blushed prettily.

'Now I want to dance a couple of numbers and then do the town,' she said. 'I want to visit the Hog Waller that's owned by that nice Mr. Cruikshanks. I like him, and I like his place, which is always gay and lively.

'You would!' snorted Crane. 'That rumhole! All the tough railroaders go there, and the worst of the cowhands, who manage to sneak out of work.'

'I like it,' Mary repeated. 'And I like the Occidental, too, that's named after

Wyatt Earp s famous place in Tombstone, Arizona.'

'Another rumhole,' growled the sheriff. 'Oh, well, everybody to their taste, as the shepherd said when he kicked — I mean kissed — the sheep. I suppose I can take it, but I'll never be the same. Waiter!'

After Crane downed his snort and Slade finished his coffee, they headed for the Hog Waller, strolling along Railroad Street at a leisurely pace, listening to the continual hullabaloo of the yards and the shops, reaching the Hog Waller without mishap.

The Hog Waller was hardly as large as the Branding Pen and not so well lighted, but it was clean and always hilarious, frequented as it was by the younger cowhands and railroaders, who found the rowdy atmosphere more than to their taste than the slightly more sedate Branding Pen. As Mary said, it was always gay and colorful, and the bartenders, floormen, and waiters were good at holding down trouble and were plagued by little more than mild ruckuses.

Jonathan Cruikshanks, the owner, was a wondrously fat man and, as fat men are always supposed to be but sometimes are not, he was jolly, smiles continually wreathing his rubicund countenance.

'Well! Well!' he boomed in a voice like thunder gobbling from a cave. 'Hide the marked decks, boys, stop putting snake juice in the redeye, clobber that roulette wheel! The Law is among us!'

'He acts like he's joking, but he ain't,' said the sheriff. 'If it wasn't that I want to keep him on display as a horrible example, I'd have closed this rumhole long ago. How are you, John?'

'Fine! Fine!' rumbled Cruikshanks. 'Nothing to complain about. Plenty of business. Lots of nice folks to 'sociate with. They — '

'Uh-huh, that crowd at the bar looks it,' the sheriff broke in sarcastically. 'I'm getting the shivers already.'

'Sit down, folks, and have a few helpin's on the house,' invited the hospitable owner. 'Hi, Miss Mary! So you brought 'em in to see old John, eh? Nice of you, plumb nice,' He beckoned a waiter to take their orders and waddled to the end of the bar to superintend the chore in person. Crane glanced around the room.

'Hmmm! Something like old home week,' he remarked, 'There's Bertram Clag, the oilman, down at the end of the bar talking with Cruikshank, And Haley Welch, the carter, up this way. Welch bellers almost as loud as Jonathan. Clag never raises his voice. Both okay, though. We could use more like them,' Slade nodded, but did not comment further.

Cruikshanks waddled back to the table, convoying a waiter bearing bottles and glasses.

'Snorts of redeye, without snake juice, for the sheriff and Mr. Slade and Mr. Lerner,' he said. 'I'll have one with you to show you it ain't pizen. Wine for the lady, and keep 'em all coming. Be seeing you in a little while, folks.' He returned to the far end of the bar.

Another familiar face appeared, Cale

Saxon, Mary's head carter, pushed through the swinging doors. He waved to Slade and his companions and sauntered to the far end of the bar, where he engaged Cruikshank, and Bertram Clag, the oil company representative, in conversation. He also had a rather loud voice, and Slade's keen ears caught most of what he was telling Cruikshanks.

'Just finished checking the carts for the Gato run,' he said. 'A big train this time. Had to take over some of the Tumble carts, Big loads, too. They'll roll in the morning, reach Gato before dark, unload the shipment, pick up their collection, and with no bad luck, make it back here some time day after tomorrow. Lots of business nowdays. Not doing bad yourself.' The conversation began dealing with the liquor business. Slade regarded Saxon thoughtfully, the concentration furrow deepening between his black brows.

A few minutes later, Bertram Clag departed, Cruikshanks walking with him to the swinging doors, then returning to

Slade's table.

'A smart feller,' he remarked, jerking his head toward the doors Clag just passed through. 'Knows his business.'

'He certainly does,' Lerner chimed in. wouldn't you say so, Walt?'

'Undoubtedly an able man,' Slade replied. Mary shot him a quick glance, a little pucker between her own slender brows, but *El Halcón* did not comment further.

Shortly, Haley Welch also took his leave. 'Got to roll west tomorrow, and a lot of spots to cover,' he explained. 'Good night, everybody.'

'Another up-and-coming gent,' observed Cruikshanks. 'Decidedly,' Slade agreed, with a slight smile that earned him another glance from Mary, and a puzzled glower from the sheriff.

Lerner and the sheriff accompanied Cruikshanks to the bar to speak with some acquaintances. Mary, who knew his every mood, regarded Slade.

'Well?' she asked.

'Well, frankly I don't know,' the Ranger

replied. 'But one thing I do know: Saxon talks too much.'

'My sentiments exactly,' Mary said. 'I'll have a word or two to say to him.'

Both knew well the casual conversation that followed was but a cover-up for their thoughts.

The Hog Waller was gay, colorful, noisy, and a bit rowdy, but everything considered, quite well behaved.

Cruikshanks rolled back to the table, chuckling, and eased his massive form carefully into a chair.

'Funny how the presence of a nice woman tones down the boys,' he said. 'Let somebody cut loose a little bad language and the 'Sh-shusses' run down the bar like escaping steam,'

'I fear you overestimate my appeal, Uncle Jonathan,' Mary replied laughingly.

'Not a bit of it!' Jonathan thunderbumbled. 'It's so!'

'And for that,' Mary said, 'you are going to get what's usually reserved for the Branding Pen. She jumped to her feet and danced across to the little raised platform that accommodated the really good Mexican orchestra and spoke with the leader, who bowed low and smiled delightedly. Seizing a guitar, he brandished it at Slade.

'*Señoritas* and *Señores*,' he shouted. 'Attention, please, and silence: *El Halcón* will sing!'

The carters, who had heard Slade sing before, cut loose a joyous bellow.

Shaking his head reprovingly at Mary, Slade crossed to the platform and accepted the guitar, which he saw at a glance was a fine instrument. He played a prelude of rolling arpeggios and ringing chords, flashed the white smile of *El Halcón* at his expectant audience, and sang, his great golden baritone-bass pealing and thundering through the room.

Songs the railroaders and the cowboys loved: the staccato boom of the exhaust, the mellow whistle note, the crash of steel on steel, sunshine and peace and the lonely stars, the thud and grumble and the marching herd and the gray terror of the stampede. All passed in review, brought before his hearers by the magic of a great voice.

For the dance-floor girls, and the girl who waited, a wistful tone-poem of his own composing that brought dainty handkerchiefs into play.

Slade had noted that Bertram Clag, the oil representative, had returned. He stood gazing at the tall singer, a haunted look in his pale eyes, his lips moving.

6

Returning the guitar to its owner with a word of thanks in Spanish, Slade made his way back to the table, with salvos of applause shaking the rafters.

'That was fine,' said Cruikshanks, wagging his big head. 'Plumb fine. Worth losing a whole night's sleep to hear. Much obliged Miss Mary, for a real treat. Got to get back to work.' He waddled off.

Suddenly Slade uttered an exclamation, tapping the tabletop with his fingers.

'Now what?' Mary asked.

'I've got it!' he replied.

'Hope it isn't catching,' said Mary. 'Just what have you got?'

'The answer to something I've been puzzling over since I retrieved that slip of paper with the plat of a trail on it from the dead store robber's belongings,' Slade explained. 'I was confident that I was familiar with the terrain over which the trail was shown as running, but where or what kept eluding me. Saxon's talk brought it to mind. It is a plat of the old short-cut trail from here to Gato, the silver town, the trail the carts will follow tomorrow.'

'And do you think somebody might make a try for the money the carts will be packing back from Gato?'

'I don't know, but I think it possible,' Slade replied.

'Then you'll ride with the carts tomorrow?' Mary asked.

Slade shook his head.

'If I ride at all, it will be day after tomorrow, early, so I'll be able to intercept the carts on the way back here.' He glanced toward where Lerner and the sheriff were still conversing with the Tumble carters at the bar.

'Please don't mention what I told you,' he said. 'If I do try to horn in on the picture, I prefer to handle the chore alone. Be safer that way, and perhaps do some good.'

'I won't mention it,' she promised, with a sigh. 'Another case of the jitters for me,' she added. 'I can feel them coming on right now. And day after tomorrow I must ride with the other train to Tumble. But I'll be back in Sanderson the next day.'

'And I'll be seeing you,' he promised in turn.

Crane and Lerner returned from the bar. Mary glanced at the clock.

'It's late and I'm growing tired,' she said. 'Don't you think it's time to leave?'

'My sentiments exactly,' replied the sheriff. 'How about it, Walt? Lerner is spending the night at my place.'

'I think it's a good idea,' Slade agreed.

'And thank you for a very pleasant evening, Uncle Jonathan,' Mary said.

'And thank *you* for the pleasure of your company,' Cruikshanks answered. 'Please come again, folks, and soon.' They promised to do so.

Parting company with Lerner and the sheriff, Mary and Slade walked slowly under the glittering stars, toward the Regan House, where the sleepy desk clerk didn't bat an eye.

Before leaving the Hog Waller, Slade had glanced around the room. Bertram Clay was not in sight.

★ ★ ★

The next day passed without incident, and the evening. But a little past midnight found Slade riding south. He did not follow the familiar trail through Persimmon Cap but an old and little-known track he had discovered that pierced the Santiagos and slithered through canyons and gorges and gulleys to reach the silver town. The trail the carts had taken.

There was a late moon in the sky, and before his eyes was spread a panorama of desolate beauty. The mountain crests were crowned with silver flame, their mighty shoulders swathed in royal purple, with farther down shadowy ebon, moon-flecked. A stretch of desert was edged in saffron.

Lonely, bleak, and ominous this land of great distances, flinging its challenge to all who would dare its savage forces of nature, its savage beasts and still more savage men. Outlaw land! Where men died, ofttimes in horrible fashion. But with an allure all its own for the adventurous spirit that dared its fastnesses and found, sometimes, contentment and peace.

Walt Slade was such a spirit. He looked upon this land as his land that had taken him for its own.

'Well, Shadow,' he said to the horse, 'here we go playing another hunch. May be but a wild goose chase where there aren't any ducks or geese, but then again, maybe not. I'm pretty well convinced the devils are going to make a try for the cart money. Whoever drew the plat must have studied the trail thoroughly and not just to pass the time away.

'Of one thing I am certain; if they do make a try it will be at least twenty miles this side of Gato. They wouldn't risk it any closer, not with the comings and goings in and from the town. But between fifteen and twenty miles out of Cato this trail forks with the well-known and heavily traveled trail to Sanderson. Hardly anybody ever rides this snake track, although it is many miles the shorter route. And just about twenty miles from Gato is a marking on the plat that I feel sure designates where the try will be made. And incidentally, there are two more markings about three hundred yards apart and around four hundred yards south of the designated marking. What they mean I haven't the slightest idea, although I feel certain they have a definite meaning, one that dovetails somehow with a spot marked for the attempt. Well, we'll see. June along, horse, and stop fussing.'

Shadow, who wasn't fussing, snorted derisively but, being well aware there were oats in one of his rider's saddle pouches, stepped out briskly, doubtless figuring that the sooner he got his loco master to wherever in blazes he was headed for, the sooner a helpin' from that pouch.

It was still dark when Slade reached the point where he believed the attempt, if one were really planned, would be made, where the trail ran through tall and thick stands of chaparral. Being familiar with the terrain, he sought out and mounted a little brush-grown, Hat-topped knoll, from the crest of which he would have a view of the trail for quite some distance in both directions. He flipped out the bit, loosened the cinches, and spread Shadow's provender, with which the big black at once occupied himself. 'Then he curled up on his blanket and went to sleep.

Dawn was flushing the east with rose and gold and birds were beginning to sing when he awoke to partake of a couple of sandwiches from one of the pouches, washing them down with a canteen of still slightly warm coffee. Shadow got a swig from a canteen of water. Confident there was no danger of being observed, Slade rolled a cigarette and smoked in leisurely comfort. It would be several hours before the carts could be expected to arrive. He stretched out on the blanket and drowsed for a while longer. Finally he glanced at the sun, arose, and moved to the lip of the crest, well screened by a straggle of growth, and stood at gaze, his eyes fixed on the trail to the south. Below where he stood, the track ran through a stand of chaparral where the outriders would have to close in on the train, bunching behind it.

'Here they come, Shadow,' he said at length, keeping his voice down. 'They're sifting sand, too, and look all set for business. How it's going to be worked I'm darned if I know, but I'm certain now the devils are down there in the brush on the far side of the trail; I'm sure I saw the top of a bush sway a trifle, as if somebody brushed against the trunk. Stay close beside me, horse; may need you.'

On came the cart train, and the drivers and outriders certainly looked to be very much on the alert.

Now the carts were close, not more than fifty yards from opposite where Slade stood, the outriders bunched behind the rearmost vehicle.

Suddenly from the crest of a hill some three or four hundred yards to the front of the train came the clang of a rifle. Instantly it was echoed from the crest of another hill only a few score of paces from the other. Followed a fusillade of shots, back and forth, back and forth from hill crest to hill crest.

The carts had jerked to a halt. Drivers and outriders stared at the two hills, exclaiming, gesturing, their attention fixed. To all appearances it was a rip-roaring corpse and cartridge session between two outfits holed up on the respective hills.

And El Halcón *understood!*

He was swinging into the saddle as half a dozen men bulged from the growth beside the trail, guns trained on the carters and outriders. Slade's voice rang out, 'Trail, Shadow, trail!'

Down the slope charged the great black horse, weaving and slithering as he had been taught to do. The distance was not too great for sixgun work, and Slade was shooting with both Colts.

An outlaw fell. Another reeled sideways, staggered, and went down. Their companions, caught utterly by surprise, confused, whirled to return the fire of the charging horseman.

The diversion was all the carters needed. They went for their holsters, blazed away at the owlhoots as fast as they could squeeze trigger.

In a moment it was over. All six owlhoots were on the ground, the maddened carters continuing to pour lead into the prostrate forms.

But a bullet fanned Slade's face as rifles boomed atop the two hills; he was in plain view of the raiders holed up on the crests.

'But I've got you ranged,' he muttered as he flicked his Colts into their sheaths, whipped out his high-power Winchester, and sent slugs whistling into the growth on the crests.

On the nearest hilltop a man hurst through the growth, cleared the lip of the crest and went tumbling and rolling down the slope. Slade sprayed each hilltop with lead. He was sure that to his keen ears came a sound of thudding hoofs fading into the distance.

The raving carters were still shooting at the dead men on the ground, cursing between shots. Slade's great voice rolled to still the tumult.

'Hold it!' he shouted. 'You're just wasting ammunition. Can't you see they're all done for?'

Wild whoops and a waving of hands greeted his approach as Shadow's irons clashed on the trail.

'Mr. Slade! Man, oh man, it's good to see you!' one bawled. 'And even better a minute ago. Thought we were goners! So you outsmarted the hellions again, eh? Yep, thought we were goners.'

Slade didn't argue the point, being of a similar opinion. Very likely the outlaws would have left no witnesses. He gazed at the distant hilltops and shook his head.

'A brand new one,' he said. 'I never heard tell of the like.'

'And if it wasn't for you, it would have worked,' declared the carter. 'We were just like so many settin' quail. Man, oh man!'

'Anyhow, altogether we made a clean sweep,' said another.

Slade shook his head.

'One or more got away,' he replied. 'And I'm ready to wager that one was the brains of the outfit. Oh, well, maybe better luck next time.'

'I figure us fellows have had our plumb share of luck today,' the head man of the carters declared fervently.

'All right, have it your way,' Slade laughed. 'Now load those bodies onto the carts. We'll stop and fish the other one out of the brush.'

The chores were quickly accomplished and the carts rolled on.

7

Despite the delay occasioned by the thwarted robbery attempt, it was not much past dark when they reached Sanderson. Soon the railroad town was seething with excitement. The bodies were packed to the sheriff's office and that flabbergasted peace officer regaled with a lurid account of how they were collected.

'Was just as if he'd dropped from the sky,' one said, apropos of Slade's dramatic appearance on the scene. 'Wouldn't have looked better to us fellers at that minute if he had. We figured we were goners for sure.'

'You very likely would have been if he hadn't showed up when he did,' growled Crane. 'It's a killer bunch.'

'Well, them seven ain't going in for any more killing unless they 'low such things in hell,' was the answer.

'Where is the young hellion?' the sheriff asked.

'Went to stable his cayuse, said he'd see you in a little while,' replied the carter. 'Come on, boys, we got things to do.'

They stored the carts, cared for their horses, and then descended on the Branding Pen in a body. And very quickly the Branding Pen was a simulacrum of Bedlam or some other madhouse on a busy day.

'So you raised hell and shoved a chunk under a corner, eh?' the sheriff greeted Slade.

'Was something like that for a while,' the Ranger admitted. 'But it cooled down fast once the carters got going. They took care of most of the devils.'

'They'd have been taken care of theirselves if it weren't for you,' Crane declared. 'How in blazes did you come to figure what was going to happen?'

'From that plat,' Slade replied. 'Once it came to me that it was a plat of the old shortcut trail, the rest was simple. The markings showed precisely where the try would be made, I resolved to be there before the carts, which I was. The two hilltop markings had me puzzled. I was confident they had an important meaning, but just what I couldn't for the life of me figure. As a result, I was very nearly caught flatfooted when what appeared to be a riproaring gun fight between a couple of rival factions holed up on those hills cut loose.'

'Very nearly, but not quite,' the sheriff observed drily.

'Go on.'

'So the outlaws were caught sort of by surprise and deflected their attention from the carters long enough to let *them* get going.'

'Uh-huh, but if it weren't for your brains and gun hands they, as they said themselves, would have been goners instead of getting going.'

'Possibly,' Slade smiled. 'But that stunt on the hilltops was a brand-new wrinkle. Never heard tell of the like, and it came very near working. Typical of the brainy individual heading the owlhoot bunch.'

'Yep, he's brainy, all right, whoever the devil he is, but my money is still on

El Halcón's brains,' Crane said cheerfully. 'How about the Branding Pen and something to eat?'

'All I've had the past twenty-four hours was two sandwiches,' Slade obliquely agreed.

As they neared the Branding Pen, Crane swore in exasperation.

'Listen to the hellions yell!' he snorted. 'They've gone plumb loco! Oh, well, after looking across into Eternity and seeing it wasn't far, I reckon they've got a right to make a little noise. Brace yourself!'

When they entered, the din redoubled, with whoops and yells and a clapping of hands. The carters surged forward, but Hardrock and his floormen, in solid phalanx, escorted them to their table and by sheer bellowing got something like order, and the two peace officers were able to enjoy their dinner without interruption.

'Mary's train rolled for Tumble early,' the sheriff observed. 'She didn't look happy. Betcha she'll be back tomorrow ahead of the carts.'

'Could be,' Slade conceded.

'She gave Saxon a wiggin' for talking too much,' Crane added as he ordered another slug of redeye. 'Do you figure it was because of his gabbin' that the try was made for the Gato train?'

'I wouldn't say for sure, but I fear the wrong pair of ears were listening when he spoke of the train rolling the next day,' Slade replied. 'Somebody must have planned that attempt quite a while ago, whoever it was that made the plat of the trail, but Saxon's talking out of turn, mentioning the train would be packing the money paid for the cartloads of materials, could have triggered the try. Was in the nature of an open invitation to do so.'

'Chances are you're right,' growled Crane.

'Well, anyhow, it didn't work and that's all that really counts,' Slade said.

'And also it gave the hellion who planned it a real notion of what it means to go up against *El Halcón*. Seven of his homed toads at a clip! Don't see how he can stand much more of that.'

'Oh, he can get replacements, perhaps not as competent as those he lost, but able to carry on. Not much of a chore in this section.'

'No mistake about that,' Crane agreed. 'The section is swarming with the ornery scuts. Well, hadn't we better mosey to the office and give those carcasses a once-over? Folks will want a look at them. I told the deputy to keep everybody out until we got back from eating.'

'Guess we might as well,' Slade answered. 'And before long, I aim to call it a day; only a few hours of half-sleep last night, and tomorrow's another day.'

'With very likely some more hell bustin' loose,' grumbled the sheriff. 'Let's go!'

With their ears ringing from the whooped goodnights of the carters, they departed.

With the door locked and the blinds drawn, they examined the bodies, Slade giving particular attention to the hands.

'Four were once cowhands, quite a while ago; the other three never were,' was his diagnosis. 'What were they? The devil only knows, although the oil-impregnated lint in the pocket seams of two appears to indicate they spent some time around the drilling field, which is interesting.'

'Might have been looking over things there to line up on something to raid,' grunted Crane.

'It is possible,' Slade conceded.

The pockets revealed nothing else Slade felt was of significance.

'About enough money to plant 'em,' said the sheriff. 'I've a notion the hellions are getting a mite short of spending cash, which I reckon means trouble for us.'

'Definitely,' Slade agreed. 'They'll hit somewhere soon.'

'And it's up to us to get the jump on the devils and figure in advance just what it will be, eh?'

'Definitely again,' Slade answered. 'And it will likely be something of a chore,'

'Oh, you'll figure it in plenty of time,

just like you did the try for the carts money,' Crane replied airily. 'No doubt in my mind of that.'

'Nice to have you so confident,' Slade smiled. 'Well, we'll see. Now you might as well open the door and let folks in. Quite a crowd collected outside.'

'They would!' the sheriff snorted as he flung open the door. 'Get set to answer fool questions.'

The crowd on the street shoved and shouldered in, chattering like a Hock of magpies. As Crane predicted, Slade was bombarded with demands for details of what happened. He answered as best he could, but soon had enough of the praise with which he was showered. Finally he escaped by explaining that he'd had but a couple of hours of sleep the night before and was going to bed. Which he proceeded to do, leaving the sheriff and the deputy to the tender mercy of the crowd, a number of which insisted they had seen one or more of the devils in town but recalled little concerning them or their doings. Which was what the Ranger expected.

Slade went to bed in a fairly satisfied frame of mind; things hadn't worked out too bad. He awoke in the early morning greatly refreshed and ready for anything, but restless.

As he ate his breakfast in the Branding Pen with only a waiter to keep him company, the restlessness refused to down. In fact it intensified. Moreso as he smoked an after-breakfast cigarette.

Finally he gave up trying to combat it, got the rig on Shadow, and rode east by slightly south at a fast pace.

It was another beautiful day, the vast reaches of the prairie flooded with golden sunshine, the amethyst-tipped grass heads swaying and rippling in a brisk wind. A day to quicken one's pulses, glad to be alive. Even the distant hills looked more companionable, less austere.

South and west the mountains shouldered the sky. In the far distances, beyond even *El Halcón*'s range of vision, the Bullis Gap Range, the Haymonds, the Pena Blanca Range, Woods Hollow

Mountains; more to the north the spired mass of the Glass Mountains; to the southwest, Cathedral Mountain.

Beyond his physical range of vision, but not his mind's eye. They were there, he knew, stem, immutable, stepping stones to Eternity. He rode on.

Soon he saw a dark smudge rising against the horizon, which he knew marked the site of Tumble, the oil town. A little later and he could bear the creaking of the walking-beams, the thud of the drills, and the cheerful puffing of the hoisting engines. There are few sounds more sprightly than those put forth by a busy oil field Here was the great Spindletop field at Beaumont in miniature.

'All we need, horse,' he said, 'is the Crosby House, the hangout of the oil millionaires and others; and Hardrock Hogan's Branding Pen Two is a fair substitute, again in miniature. Well, we haven't met anybody on the way, which means that Mary hasn't gotten away yet, Reckon she'll be a mite surprised when we show up. Think she'll be glad to see us?'

Shadow's snort was noncommittal. Slade chuckled and tweaked his ear. Shadow bared teeth as white and even as Slade's own, and barely grazed his overalls. And would have done a lot more than graze, had Shadow really meant business. They understood each other perfectly, Slade and his one-man horse.

She was glad to see them, her eyes showed it, when they found her at the cart station, checking the loads, but all she said was, 'Well! This is indeed a surprise. So you actually came looking for me once.'

'I just came for the ride,' he replied airily, and hugged her close.

'Was there a real reason for your riding down here?' she asked, her eyes suddenly anxious.

'No,' he answered, 'I just felt restless, that's all.'

'And that, you being restless, spells trouble,' she sighed. 'But anyway, you're here, and that's what really counts.'

'And I'm glad to be here,' he said.

'And that counts, too,' she smiled. 'I'll finish checking before long and we'll have dinner together.'

'I'll care for my horse and meet you in Branding Pen Two. How's Lerner?'

'He's all right, conferring with well owners relative to what they'll want for the next cart loads. They never seem to get all they need. The loads will be ready as soon as the empties reach Sanderson.'

'But all in all, you're on the way to being a very wealthy woman,' Slade remarked.

''Put not your trust in material things'.'

'No, but material things can be put to a good use and by so doing cease to be *material* things.'

'That is your philosophy, I know, and you practice it,' Mary said.

'And so do such men as Westbrook Lerner, Jaggers

Dunn, and others,' Slade pointed out. 'Yes.'

Slade stabled his horse, chatted for a while with the old Mexican keeper, then repaired to Branding Pen Two, sat down and waited for Mary.

Abruptly his attention fixed for a moment. Standing at the bar sipping a drink was the oil company representative, Bertram Clag.

However, he recalled the sheriff mentioning that Clag spent quite a bit of time in Tumble. Which, the nature of his employment taken into consideration, was not surprising. He noted that at the moment, Clag's attention was focused on the swinging doors, through which Mary Merril had entered.

'Got away sooner than I expected to,' she announced breathlessly. 'Mr. Lerner took over when I told him you were in town. Nice of him, wasn't it?'

'It certainly was,' Slade agreed.

'Or do you resent me traipsing around after you like I'm doing?' she said, slanting him a glance through her lashes.

'Just one similar remark and I'll shock the gathering,' he threatened, half rising from his chair.

'I'll be good! I'll be good!' Mary exclaimed hurriedly.

8

Lerner arrived before they finished eating. He said a word to the head bartender, and he and that dignitary entered the back room together, to reappear shortly, Lerner joining Slade and Mary.

'All set to roll come morning,' he announced after giving a waiter his order. 'Money' stashed in the safe, where it'll *be* safe.'

During the meal Slade was silent and distrait. Mary watched him anxiously. She knew that look. Knew he was pursuing something up and down the channels of his mind.

But she asked no questions. She knew he would talk to her when he was ready, not before. Questions would just irritate him, and she was too wise a bit of fluff to do that.

So she chatted gaily with Lerner, who appeared to be in a very satisfied mood and optimistic of the future.

'Put down two more wells in the past two days,' he said. 'What do you think of the pool now, Mr. Slader?'

'I haven't revised my original opinion,' Slade replied. 'But I do think it will continue producing for quite some time yet.'

'That makes for good listening,' chuckled Lerner. 'Will help out quite a few folks who can use help.'

'And you,' Slade predicted smilingly, 'will soon be off in search of fresh pastures. It's in your blood.'

'And I fear *he'll* be off in search of fresh pastures, and I'm not referring to oil wells,' Mary sighed.

'I'm maligned,' Slade insisted, and again lapsed into the silence both his companions respected.

The night closed down, calm and peaceful, glittered by stars, and Tumble's hum and clatter seemed to louden in the great silence of the plains, an oasis of activity sur rounded by the vast quiet.

The carters boomed in, waving and shouting, and business picked up fast.

'You'd think they'd crave a little rest,

but not them,' Mary remarked. 'They'll be going strong until I route them off to bed.'

Slade spoke. 'I think I'll mosey over to the sheriff's branch office and have a word or two with Deputy Charley Blount,' he said. 'He should be in about now.'

'Here we go again!' sighed Mary. 'Oh, I know it's only a couple of blocks from here, but that's plenty to give you an opportunity to get mixed up in something. Be seeing you, dear.'

As he shouldered his way along the crowded, uproarious street, Slade was inclined to agree with Mary that the two blocks could well provide opportunity for most anything.

However, nothing out of the way happened and he reached the office without mishap, where he was warmly welcomed by Deputy Blount.

'Well, Charley, how goes it?' he asked after they shook hands and Blount had procured steaming coffee from the stove in the back room.

'Not so good,' the deputy replied. 'Seems the bunch that is operating around Sanderson, or another one just as bad, is cutting loose here, too. Several robberies, a couple of killings, three chores of burgling. Most of the spreads to the east of here swear they're losing cows; reckon they are. Oh, it's the same old story, a boom town attracting all the riffraff between Beaumont and El Paso.'

'That's covering considerable territory, but I understand what you mean,' Slade smiled. 'After we finish our coffee, you may give me some details, and if you've any notion of something that might be pulled in the near future.'

'The saloon robberies were pulled in just about the way they were at Sanderson,' Blount said. 'Devils slipped in through back room doors that were supposed to be locked. One time they didn't kill anybody, other time they shot the owner who was tallying the week's take. Stores were burgled mighty slick, holes bored in safe doors. Was a night watchman on duty in one place. He got his head spilt open by a gun barrel, didn't kill him.'

Blount paused a moment, evidently turning something over in his mind

''Pears the widelooped cows were run to the river and across,' he resumed. 'One guarded herd lost a cowhand. Found what was left of him by a waterhole where the critters had been bedded down. Guess he never had a chance. Owners have been patrolling their holdings but without any luck.'

Slade nodded, unscrambling the deputy's rambling monologue, which wasn't hard to do, his account following a familiar pattern.

'Any money shipments that might provide the owlhoots with opportunity?' he asked. Blount pondered.

'Darned if I can think of anything,' he confessed. 'The week's takes usually go by way of Miss Merril's carts, and they're just a mite too well guarded to put notions into the heads of gents with share-the-wealth ideas. Otherwise it goes in saddle pouches with two or three straight-shooting jiggers to guard it. There are no stages here, as you know, and money from the east most always goes straight through to Sanderson to be apportioned. Very seldom if ever anything on the short-line train from the junction. It — hey! wait a minute! Just thought of something they were discussin' at the railroad station. There is a hefty poke of *dinero* coming in on the late train, which gets here a bit past midnight. Seems that oil company feller Bertram Clag figures to buy a couple of wells over at the west edge of the field that are producing fairly good but nothing to write home about. Gather he figures to sink deeper wells against the chance of hitting a pool beneath this one. 'Pears to believe it'll work.'

'He might have something there,' Slade said thoughtfully. 'Happened at Beaumont. Go on.'

'So Clay is having a lot of money sent to him here from Brownsville, I believe, the well owners wanting cash. The station agent was instructing a coupla jiggers who were to be at the station to receive it. That give you any notions?'

'It might,' Slade said even more thoughtfully. For some minutes he sat silent, then abruptly stood up.

'Charley,' he said, 'stick around the office or Branding Pen Two until I come back. I may be gone some little while.'

'I'll do it, Mr. Slade,' the deputy promised. Slade nodded and hurried out the door. He made straight for Shadow's stable and cinched up swiftly.

'Okay, feller, we're in for a little leg stretching,' he told the horse as he led him from the stable and swung into the saddle.

Shadow, who had a decided liking for leg stretching, snorted gaily.

'But you're liable to have to sift sand before this is over,' Slade warned. Shadow snorted even more gaily and quickened his pace a little.

After passing the oil field and the assembly yard, Slade rode almost due south. He rode warily, scanning each clump of brush, each stand of chaparral, although he did not really anticipate trouble in the course of the ride. When he reached his destination, which was the junction of the road with the east-west line, it might very well be different. He rode paralleling the railroad but keeping well back from the steel.

'Well, horse, here goes playing another hunch and hoping it's a straight one,' he observed.

The hunch, so called, was in fact a carefully detailed analysis of the situation as it stood, and endeavoring to put himself in the outlaws' place and reacting as they would, for which he had an unique and proven ability to do. Thinking as they could be expected to think, and governing his own actions accordingly. Outthinking the devils as well as outshooting them, as Captain McNelty would say.

If a try for the money was planned, he did not believe it would be put into effect at the Tumble station. There were always people around the station, and the two men assigned the duty of receiving the money were express company employees trained against emergencies. In his opinion the attempt would be made at the junction of the shortline road with the east-west line, where the money would be transferred from the Westbound Flyer to the shortline road. He knew he could be wrong, of course, but if so, there was nothing he could do about it. He could only follow the dictates of his own judgment and hope for the best.

His paramount problem at the moment was to reach the junction ahead of the Flyer, so he steadily increased Shadow's pace until the great horse was going at racing speed. While he anxiously gazed eastward for the firs headlight gleam and his ears strained to catch the faint whistle note that would herald the approach of the mainline train.

To the fact that he was embarked on a very hazardous undertaking he gave no thought. He was thankful that the weather had decided to give him a break. The sky that had been so clear when he started out was now heavily overcast, the night very dark, with even large objects visible for only a short distance, even to the eyes of *El Halcón*.

Which was all to the good. The gloom would veil his approach, and Shadow's irons made only a whisper of sound on the heavy grass.

From far away in the depths of the night came a thin whistle wail. Another moment and there was a faint flicker of light in the east. Slade estimated the distance he still had to cover, the time it would take the Flyer to reach the junction. His voice rang out:

'Trail, Shadow! Trail!'

Instantly the great horse extended himself still more, his flying hoofs spurning the soil. He snorted, blew through his nose and literally poured his long body over the ground. Slade stared anxiously at the steadily brightening headlight beam.

'She's going to beat us, but not much,' he muttered.

Bell clanging, brake shoes grinding the tires, the Flyer roared up to the junction. Almost instantly sounded a crackle of gunfire and a wild yelling. Another minute and through a straggle of brush crashed Shadow, skating to a halt, his rider leaving the saddle while the horse was in full stride, keeping his balance by a miracle of agility.

Slade took in the situation at a glance. The Tumble train's express messenger lay motionless on the ground. A man was holding a gun on the Flyer's engineer. Two more were shooting at the coaches to keep the passengers inside. A fourth man was leaping from the Flyer's express car, a couple of plump pokes under one arm, a gun in his other hand. He gave a yelp of alarm and the gun blazed, the slug fanning the ducking, dodging Ranger's face. The others whirled in his direction. Slade's voice thundered as he shot with both hands:

'Up! You are under arrest!'

The man with the pokes was the first to fall, pitching forward onto his face. Slade whipped his guns around and poured lead at the pair beside the coaches. One fell, his scream of agony echoing the roar of Slade's Colts. Answering bullets ripped Slade's overalls, ribboned his shirt sleeve, just grazing the flesh of his left arm. The second coach attacker steadied himself, lined sights with *El Halcón's* breast.

But before he could squeeze trigger, he died, riddled by Slade's bullets.

The man holding the gun on the Flyer's engineer whipped around the front of the engine and vanished from sight as the hammers of Slade's guns clicked on empty shells. With a mutter of disgust he slipped in a couple of fresh cartridges and dashed after the fugitive outlaw.

But as he rounded the front of the locomotive, he heard fast hoofs beating the trail, to fade westward. The last of the raiders had escaped.

A glance told *El Halcón* there was nothing more to be feared from the others; they were quite satisfactorily dead. He saw what he had hardly noted during the excitement of the encounter, that all were partly masked by neckerchiefs drawn high, almost to the eyes.

The Flyer's express messenger, as to whose fate Slade had been apprehensive, appeared in the doorway, yammering incoherently, his eyes wild and staring.

'Shut up!' Slade told him in a voice that got instant obedience. 'Get down here and collect these money pokes. Check and make sure the contents are intact, while I give your Tumble colleague a once-over,' The messenger obeyed orders. Slade turned to the other messenger. His fears for him were allayed when he saw he was sitting up rubbing his head and grinning.

'Was just heading to tie onto the Tumble poke when a devil slipped in behind me and walloped me one with a gun barrel,' he explained, leaping to his feet. 'My cap cushioned the blow, I reckon. Knocked me down but not out. I sorta played 'possum against the chance he'd give me another one. Stayed that way while shootin' was going on. Figured it the best thing to do.'

'It was,' Slade agreed. 'Quite likely

saved your life. Now take over the Tumble poke, make sure it's okay, and onto your train.'

Now the Flyer's train crew, followed by chattering, questioning passengers, were streaming from the coaches.

'Herd them back inside and get going,' Slade told the Flyer's conductor. 'There's nothing you can do here and you're late already.'

The conductor shouted, 'All aboard!' The engineer blew two warning blasts, and the coaches began to refill.

'Looked out the window and into that hellion's gun muzzle,' he replied to Slade's question. 'The devil ordered me to hold the train. I did.'

'You, too, were smart,' Slade told him. 'All right, the con is waving a highball. Get going!'

The stack boomed, the drivers spun for a moment, then gripped as the sand blowers poured sand on the rails. The Flyer roared on its belated way.

9

The Tumble train's crew, who had evidently been discreetly staying in the clear, appeared.

'Mr. Slade, you sure showed up at the right time,' said the conductor, mopping his perspiring forehead. 'Things didn't look too good.'

'Worked out quite well,' Slade conceded. 'Nobody killed except those with a killing coming, which is more than I hoped for one time. Okay, load the bodies into the express car and pack them to Tumble. Your money poke okay, messenger?'

'Just right,' the messenger replied. 'Man, oh, man! The nerve of you, tackling all four of the devils by yourself!'

'The element of surprise worked to my advantage,' Slade belittled. 'They were sort of confused.' A general laugh greeted the sally.

The bodies were loaded and the little

train puffed for Tumble.

Slade retrieved Shadow who when the shooting started had immediately gotten in the clear, flipped out the bit and loosened the cinches so the cayuse could quench its thirst at a trickle of water that ran nearby and crop a few mouthfuls of grass. Then he ranged the chaparral that fringed the far side of the east-west line right-of-way, located the three outlaw horses tethered to tree trunks and removed the rigs, leaving them to fend for themselves until picked up. The afternoon train could pack the rigs to town.

It was far past broad daylight when Slade reached Tumble. He cared for his horse and then repaired to Branding Pen Two where, as he expected, Mary was waiting for him. With her, to his surprise, was Sheriff Crane. Mary sighed relief, the sheriff glowered.

'Knew darn well you were going to tangle with something when you lit out without saying anything to anybody,' he said. 'That's why I took a sudden notion to amble down this way. So give us the straight of it. The train crew said you chased a dozen more 'sides the three you did for. Sounded reasonable.'

'A slight exaggeration, I fear,' Slade smiled. 'Guess they were excited and saw double, or triple, as the case might be.'

'Well, thank goodness, you weren't hurt,' Mary said.

'But I see I have a chore of shirt and overalls to patch.' 'Better have him take 'em off,' suggested the sheriff.

'Oh, he'll take them off. He — confound you and your sly remarks, Uncle Tom! Always a double entendre!'

'Whatever that means,' the sheriff returned blithely. 'Guess it fits. Well, here comes Walt's helpin'. As he would say, the cook sorta anticipated.'

Although the day was still early, Branding Pen Two was already well crowded, the thwarted robbery the chief topic of discussion. Admiring glances were bent on Slade, but the floormen would allow no one to interrupt his meal.

He had finished eating and was enjoying a smoke when Bertram Clag, the oil company representative, entered and at once approached the table.

'I'm greatly beholden to you, Mr. Slade,' he said. 'The money was, of course, insured by the express company, but the delay would have greatly inconvenienced me. I'm having trouble putting my deal across as is; the owners of wells in question can't seem to be of the same mind from one day to the next. I hope for the psychological effect of money on the table. Yes, I wish to thank you for what you did, very much.' With a smile and a nod he departed.

The sheriff watched his broad shoulders pass through the swinging doors.

'Not a bad sort, I'd say,' was his comment Slade smiled and got a quick glance from Mary.

'Guess we'd better drop over to the office and glance at the bodies,' he suggested.

'A notion,' nodded Crane. 'I locked the door and sent Blount to bed; he'd been up all night, too, waiting for you to show.'

'And then *you* go to bed,' Mary said to Slade. 'You look worn out.'

'It has been a rather tempestuous night,' the Ranger admitted.

There were quite a few of the curious hanging around the office, but Crane refused admittance to anybody for the time being.

'Not much money this time, either,' he remarked after turning out the contents of the pockets. 'Hellions ain't having much luck of late. Wouldn't be surprised if it's beginning to hurt.'

'And liable to hurt us, too,' Slade said. 'Our luck has been running unusually good of late, but the law of averages is liable to catch up with us. There'll be another try made soon.'

'We'll try 'em,' the sheriff answered cheerfully. 'Ornery looking hellions.'

'And not as intelligent appearing as the former ones,' was Slade's verdict. 'New replacements, I'd say, but the chances are still some of the original bunch are mavericking around.'

'I ain't worried,' returned Crane.

'They'll get their comeuppance just as the others have. What did you learn from the hands?'

'That two were former cowhands but the other never was,' Slade replied. 'Well, you can let folks have a look if you are of a mind to. Then I'm going to bed.'

The sheriff nodded and stood up, but lingered beside his chair, tugging his mustache — a habit with him when he was slightly uncertain about broaching a subject — seemed to make up his mind, then asked a question:

'Got any real notion yet as to who is the head devil of the bunch?'

'Yes, I have a notion,' Slade replied slowly. 'One that appears ridiculous, on the face of it. I'm not ready to talk about it just yet, for I could be making a colossal blunder.'

'Darn little chance of that,' Crane differed. 'If you've got that much of a notion, you've got the real homed toad tagged and labeled. Just a matter of time.'

'Hope you're right,' Slade said smilingly.

'Ain't in the habit of being wrong,' retorted the sheriff as he unlocked and opened the door to let the horde in. Very quickly the office was well filled.

But, at variance with other occasions, nobody could recall seeing either of the unsavory specimens before, the concensus of opinion being that they were members of the bunch operating around Sanderson and this their first appearance in the Tumble area.

'And their last,' chuckled an oldtimer. 'Reckon they hadn't heard about *El Halcón* or they'd have steered clear of this section, a bad section for owlhoots about now.'

Slade again hoped the speaker was right in his prediction. As to the contention that it was the trio's first visit to the Tumble area, he was inclined to agree.

'By the way, any notion the jigger who made it in the clear last night was the one you're paying a mind to?' asked Crane.

'I really couldn't say,' Slade replied. 'I never got a really good look at him, and I was rather busy when he made his escape around the front of the engine. One thing is sure for certain; his action evinced hairtrigger thinking and an instant grasp of opportunity. Well, we'll see. Goodnight, Tom, I'm heading for bed.'

* * *

Slade awoke to the glory of the Texas sunset feeling well rested and quite satisfied with the previous night's work. He had proven his deductions sound, his hunch a straight one, and he believed he had dealt the outlaw bunch a blow they would probably remember for some time.

He bathed, shaved, and although he was hungry, made his first stop at the sheriff's office where he found Crane smoking the pipe of peace in comfortable solitude.

'Carcasses wrapped up and in one of the carts, which will roll to Sanderson tomorrow morning,' he said, interpreting Slade's glance at the empty floor. 'Doc

Cooper will want to hold an inquest, of course. The Tumble line express messenger and a brakeman will amble along as witnesses which, with you to back 'em, will be enough to satisfy the jury. Now what?'

'Now some breakfast, dinner, or whatever you want to call it. Anyhow, something to eat.'

'Them's my sentiments,' said Crane. 'I waited to eat with you. Nothing more to do here. Maybe we can make it a couple of blocks without getting mixed up in a rukus, though you couldn't get Mary to bet on it. Let's go!'

When they reached the saloon, only Westbrook Lerner was occupying their reserved table.

'Miss Merril is in her room; said she'd be down shortly,' the head bartender reported.

The sheriff paused at the bar to speak with some acquaintances. Slade joined Lerner.

'Well, Bertram Clag appears very grateful to you for saving his money,'

Lerner remarked. Slade's reply was a monosyllable, 'Yes.'

Lerner regarded him for a moment, then, 'Walt, do you believe he really has a chance to strike a deep pool?'

'No, I don't, and neither do you,' *El Halcón* said. 'All the geological aspects are against it. Different at Spindletop, where experienced oilmen knew what to eventually expect. Such a drilling was impractical in those days, but with the improved rotary drills and other machinery advancement, the chore became simple. Here this shallow seepage pool is all.'

'But shouldn't Clag know that?' asked Lerner.

'As a representative of an oil firm he certainly should,' Slade replied.

'Then what the devil does he have in mind?' Lerner wondered.

'That's your question,' Slade answered evasively. 'Last night he intimated that he was having trouble closing his deal with the well owners.'

'A money gap, I gather,' Lerner said.

'The owners are not satisfied with the amount he offers for the wells.'

'Westbrook, do you know what oil company he represents?' Slade asked.

'The Ajax Corporation, I understand,' answered Lerner.

Slade stared at him. 'The Ajax Corporation!' he repeated.

'That's right, the Ajax Corporation. Mean something to you?'

'The Ajax Corporation,' Slade said slowly, 'is a subsidiary of the Neches Waterway outfit with which I twice had trouble at the irrigation projects near Laredo.'

'And gave them their comeuppance,' Lerner nodded. 'I heard about that. A rather off-color outfit.'

'To put it mildly,' Slade conceded. 'To that bunch, ethics is just a word in the dictionary.'

'So Clag is tangled with a crooked bunch?'

'Don't be hasty in your judgment,' Slade cautioned. 'The Neches people hire the best engineers and other experts they are able to, who do not necessarily take part in their shenanigans, which are usually at the top. And so far as the deep pool is concerned, there is a very remote possibility that we might be wrong and Clag right.'

'As to that, I'll string along with the best engineer in Texas,' Lerner said. 'If you say there ain't one, there ain't.'

Slade laughed. 'Everybody makes mistakes,' he pointed out.

'Darn few made by *El Halcón*,' Lerner grunted. 'Here comes one that sure isn't a mistake.'

It was Mary Merril, bouncing across the room to plump into a chair close to Slade's.

The sheriff joined them at the same moment. He shook his head wisely.

'A plumb good chore of patching,' he remarked, glancing at Slade's shirt and overalls.

Mary pointedly ignored him. 'I want to eat,' she said. 'Nice of you to wait for me.'

'By gosh, it is time for a small helpin'

or two,' agreed the sheriff. 'Had plumb forgot about it.'

'And then a few dances and call it an early night,' Mary added. 'I've got a busy day ahead of me tomorrow. Can't hold up the carts any longer; the drillers are yelping for supplies.'

'I'd have started them early this morning if it wasn't for you,' she said accusingly to Slade. 'I just couldn't leave Tumble until I knew for sure what, or who had happened to you.'

'Lots of 'who's' on the dance floor,' Crane chimed in blithely. Mary did not appear impressed.

10

The carts rolled early the following morning. With them rode Lerner, the sheriff, and Slade.

'If I don't let you out of my sight, perhaps you can keep out of trouble,' Mary told him as she reined Rojo, her big red sorrel, in close to Shadow.

Slade was more than usually alert on the way to Sanderson and made sure the outriders were on their toes. He did not see how they could possibly meet with trouble on the way to Sanderson, over the open prairie, but the character he was up against was too good at unexpectedly pulling rabbits from the hat to take any chances with. Every hilltop and stand of brush came in for careful scrutiny. The movements of every bird on the wing were studied. There were quite a few coyotes in the area, and as the day declined toward evening he gave heed to their yipping, listening for the barks to develop a querulous note, which would signify something was disturbing the little prairie wolves.

However, they reached Sanderson before sunset with no mishap on the way. Mary's money was stashed in the Branding Pen office safe, which was as secure as the Bank of England was supposed to be.

The carters stowed their vehicles, cared for their horses. Mary repaired to her room in the Regan House to freshen up a bit, as she put it, before eating runner. Slade domiciled Rojo, her big sorrel, in a stall next to Shadow's and enjoyed a sluice in the ice water of the trough in the rear of the stable. Much refreshed thereby, he headed for the Branding Pen.

On his way to the saloon, Slade paused to gaze toward the railroad yards. He was experiencing a disturbing premonition that the next outlaw strike would have some thing to do with the yards or the railroad. Just why he couldn't for the life of him say, but it was very real, and something he had learned not to lightly dismiss. In a very thoughtful mood he continued to the Branding Pen, to find that Lerner and the sheriff had preceded him.

Mary arrived shortly, looking fresh as a daisy, as Crane put it. And hungry, per usual.

'See?' she said. 'Stay with me all the time and you never get into trouble.'

'Worked that way today,' he admitted.

'And maybe it will work a little longer,' she said. 'Take our time at dinner, then a few dances, some chatter, and call it an early night. Can't expect the luck to hold too long, and tomorrow's another day.'

'Sounds good to me,' replied the sheriff. 'I'll have to admit I feel sorta fagged; has been a hard day.'

Lerner nodded emphatic agreement. Slade said nothing, his eyes thoughtful. Mary regarded him anxiously; she knew that look and wondered if he had learned something he preferred not to discuss at the moment. However, she shrugged daintily and addressed herself to her food. No sense in borrowing trouble.

They proceeded to put their planned

program into effect and the hours jogged along pleasantly enough. The Branding Pen was plenty busy but not particularly boisterous. Even the tired carters were somewhat subdued.

Meanwhile a little yard engine puffed cheerfully along, shoving an express car onto a siding that led to the main line. All afternoon a crew of workers had been loading express into that car. Shortly before midnight it would be coupled onto the westbound El Paso Flyer. Several workers were putting a leisurely finish to the chores.

In the car the messenger was busily working on his books. A big iron safe in the corner stood open. So far as was generally known, there was nothing of value in that safe.

Down the gravity hump rolled a string of loaded cars, destined for a siding in the lower yard. Suddenly one of the lead lights turned from white to red, denoting that a switch from the lead to a siding was open. On that siding was a string of cars.

A brakeman riding the moving string a couple of cars back gave a yelp of alarm as the wheels of the lead car ground against the points. He twirled a brake wheel madly, with no effect.

The string from the hump struck the head car of the string on the siding. There was a tremendous crash, followed almost instantly by an even more tremendous crash, followed almost instantly by an ever more tremendous roar. In the head car of the string on the siding were a dozen boxes of dynamite securely cleated to the floor, able to resist the normal bumps and jolts of travel, but not able to resist such an impact as the one to which they had been subjected. Which complicated things, decidedly.

The boxcar containing the dynamite was blown to matchwood. The whole yard was shaken by the concussion. Had the brakeman been riding the head car of the hump string, he would have assuredly been killed. As it was, he was merely knocked to the running board, blinded, his ears ringing bell notes.

In the express car, some distance from the wreck, the messenger sat rigid in his chair, slightly stunned by the force of the explosion. The loading workers, yelling, cursing, were rushing to the scene of the wreck.

The messenger scrambled to his feet, reeling drunkenly, and lurched toward the door. Before he reached it, three men — two masked, the third wearing a heavy dark beard — leaped and scrambled into the car. The messenger looked into the muzzles of leveled guns.

The bearded man jerked his gun toward the rear of the car. 'Get over there, and stay there,' he ordered. The shivering messenger obeyed, cowering against the crates and bales. One robber held a gun on him; the others sped to the open safe, smashed an inner drawer, and swiftly transferred rolls of gold coin and packets of bills into a sack held by the bearded man. In a matter of seconds they finished the chore and rushed to the door.

Last out was the bearded man. Before

leaping to the ground he turned and blazed a shot at the messenger, who gave a choking cry and fell forward onto his face.

However, the messenger was but slightly creased by the bullet. Sure the robbers were gone, he leaped from the car, yelling his loudest. But it was some little time before anybody at the scene of the explosion paid any attention to what he was trying to tell. And nobody knew what to do about it.

★ ★ ★

When the explosion rocked the Branding Pen, Slade was instantly on his feet.

'At the railroad yards,' he said. 'Come on, Tom.' He raced to the swinging doors, Crane, Lerner, and Mary Merril close behind, the bellowing Branding Pen patrons streaming after them.

'I knew it!' wailed Mary. 'I knew the night couldn't pass without something happening. I could read it in your eyes that you expected trouble.'

'Not my making,' Slade replied. 'Let's go!'

Flame was flickering over the wreckage, and clouds of acrid smoke.

'Yes, dynamite,' Slade said. 'Must have been some boxes in one of the cars.'

'When they reached the scene of the wreck, the express messenger came running to the sheriff, gabbling out his story of what happened in the express car.

'Did they get much?' Crane asked.

'They did,' answered the messenger. 'More than two thousand dollars, money consigned from the Sanderson bank to the bank in El Paso. Nobody was supposed to know it was in the car, but I guess somebody did.'

'Fairly obvious,' Slade remarked. 'I suppose the messengers brought the money to the car, right?'

'That's right,' conceded the messenger. 'This morning before daylight.'

'An open invitation to anybody who might have been curious about that car and keeping an eye on it. Well seems some people will never learn. Fortunately it would appear nobody was killed.'

'I thought I was a goner,' confessed the messenger. 'There was murder in that big devil's eyes.'

Slade did not think so; he believed the big man was just centering the messenger's attention on himself for some reason of his own. Otherwise his bullet would have done more than just touch the messenger's scalp.

'And you figure the wreck was deliberately staged?' the sheriff asked.

'Of course,' Slade replied. 'To attract everybody away from the car, which it did. The dynamite was just an unexpected additional fillip that conveniently worked into their hands. Oh, it's a smooth bunch, and they get lucky breaks.'

'If you'd known there was money in that car, they'd have got a different sort of break,' growled Crane.

'Possibly,' Slade conceded.

The yardmaster came hurrying up. 'Get in your car,' he directed the messenger. 'The Flyer's due in five minutes and that load of junk must go to El Paso, money or no money.'

The messenger obeyed. Faint with distance sounded a whistle wail. Ten minutes later the Flyer boomed west, trundling the moneyless express car.

The fire was still burning fiercely, but now the volunteer fire department was on the job, pouring water onto the flames, which they would soon have under control.

'And I reckon we might as well mosey back to the Branding Pen,' Slade said. 'Nothing we can do here.'

'Right!' agreed the sheriff. 'I can do with a couple of snorts of harmless old redeye.'

'And I'm hungry,' said Mary.

When they had reached the Branding Pen and were alone for a few minutes, Lerner asked Slade, 'Think it was a Neches Waterway job?'

El Halcón shook his head. 'They don't go in for such picayune stuff. Their notion would be to plan a scheme to try and steal the railroad.'

'The messenger said the big fellow

who appeared to be giving the orders wore whiskers,' the oilman commented thoughtfully.

'Probably a false beard,' Slade said. 'Easy to procure and so well made nowadays it is difficult to tell one from a natural growth. Chances are the next time he's seen he will be clean shaven.'

'Just what I was thinking,' Lerner said meaningly.

'Keep your thoughts to yourself,' Slade cautioned. 'You could be making a grave mistake and doing — somebody an injustice.'

'Oh, I'll keep a tight *latigo* on my jaw, as the cowhands say,' Lerner promised. 'Here come Mary and the sheriff, one, thirsty, the other hungry. Can stand a snack myself.

'I'll join you,' Slade agreed. 'As Tom would say, watching owlhoots put one over makes me hungry.'

The lack was soon cared for, and everybody agreed to call it a night.

11

The next day found Mary and Lerner loading the carts for another roll to Tumble. Slade and the sheriff sat in the latter's office and talked.

'And the devils are well heeled again, so far as money goes,' Crane remarked.

'Yes,' Slade agreed, 'but it won't last. Their sort get rid of money very fast.'

'Which means we can be on the lookout for more trouble, eh?'

'Definitely. I only hope we'll do a better chore of anticipating than last night.'

'How in blazes could you have anticipated what happened last night?' Crane demanded. 'You would have needed a little dose of the second sight your wayback Scotch ancestors claimed to have.'

'I fear the second sight is somewhat outmoded,' Slade smiled. 'But I'll have to agree that figuring last night in advance would have been a trifle difficult. But I also must admit that last night I had a premonition that something relative to the railroad was going to cut loose, but not the slightest notion as to what it could be. A hunch that wasn't a hunch, you might call it.'

'Betcha the next one will be right on the dot,' predicted Crane. 'Just watch.'

'Hope you're right,' Slade said. 'Well, we'll see. Did you have any breakfast? I didn't.'

'Nope,' replied Crane. 'I was just as anxious as you were to get to the office and see if anything was to be learned. So suppose we toddle over to the Branding Pen and choke down a bite.'

When they entered the Branding Pen, Bertram Clag, the Ajax Oil Corporation representative was standing at the bar, He waved a cordial greeting, but Slade was sure he detected an amused gleam in his pale eyes. His own eyes were thoughtful as he gave a waiter his order.

As was to be expected, the express-car robbery was being vigorously discussed.

'What do you say, Walt? Figure it was the same bunch that has been working the section?' Hardrock Hogan asked.

'I would presume so,' Slade replied. 'Had all the earmarks of their work, carefully planned and executed, with meticulous regard for details.'

'That's the way I feel about it,' said Hogan. 'Well, as Tom says, just a matter of time. As it has been before, so it will be. I'm putting my money on *El Halcón*.'

'Such confidence is inspiring,' Slade replied smilingly.

'Now what?' he added as a wild yelling and whooping sounded outside.

'Oh, that's just Haley Welch's carters rolling in from the west,' Hardrock explained. 'They're bad as Miss Merril's bunch when it comes to making a racket. We'll have 'em with us before long.'

'And the till bell will be ringing,' quoth the sheriff. 'No wonder he's grinning,' with a glance at Hardrock. 'No music so sweet as the song the till bell sings.' Hardrock grinned even broader, and declined to be drawn into an argument.

Before Slade and the sheriff finished eating, Welch's carters did appear for a snack and a drink, and business did pick up, decidedly.

Shortly, Welch himself dropped in. He waved to the sheriff and joined Bertram Clag at the bar. The pair conversed at length in low tones.

'Wonder what those jiggers find to talk about?' remarked Crane.

'Hard to tell,' Slade answered. 'Have Welch and his train ever had trouble?'

The sheriff shook his head. 'Never been bothered, so far as I've heard. Of course his carts are well guarded, with outriders on the job. Wonder he hasn't, though. It's a rough country he deals with. As you know, plenty has happened between here and Marathon and Alpine.'

'Decidedly,' Slade agreed.

At that moment Mary Merril and Lerner entered, their carters streaming after them, and the subject dropped, The noise in the Branding Pen somewhat more than doubled.

'Knocked off for a little nourishment,' Mary announced, 'The boys have been doing fine with the loading. We'll be all set to roll to Tumble tomorrow.'

'And the folks down at the field will be glad to see you,' Lerner said.

'To see me, or rather, to see the loads of casings and so forth, don't you mean?' Mary countered.

'They'll always be glad to see a beautiful woman,' Lerner replied gallantly.

'Anybody who associates with Walt quickly acquires the gift of blarney,' said Miss Merril. 'It's catching, like the sweating fever or the hives. I want to eat!'

'Guess that's catching, too,' said Lerner. 'So do I.'

After finishing their snack with a snort or two of redeye to hold it down, the carters boomed out. Shortly, Mary and Lerner followed. The driller lingered for a moment.

'Going to ride with us tomorrow, Walt?' he asked.

'Yes, I think I will,' Slade decided. 'That is, if nothing happens to cause me to change my mind.'

'I sure hope nothing happens,' Lerner said. 'I always feel a lot safer with you around; so darn many devilish things happened hereabouts of late.' He glanced toward the bar.

'Wonder what our *amigo* Bertram Clag and Haley Welch have been discussing so seriously? They're busier than a dog burying bones.'

Slade repeated his answer to a similar question from Sheriff Crane. 'Hard to tell.'

But despite his noncommittal replies, Slade was wondering a little himself as to what the oddly assorted pair might have in common. The one subtle, secretive, adroit, with a mind keen as a razor's edge. The other bluff, hearty, outspoken, easy to read, his actions not at all difficult to anticipate. Yes, a curious combination of opposites.

'A funny couple,' agreed the sheriff, who had been an attentive listener to Lerner's remarks. 'Well, reckon we'd better get back to the office and see if something else has busted loose. Wouldn't be a bit surprised if something has.'

'Would be strictly in order,' Slade

answered. As they passed through the swinging doors, he glanced toward the bar and saw that Clag and Welch were still engaged in earnest converse.

In the office, Crane glowered disapprovingly at the bare floor next to the far wall.

'Don't look right,' he complained. 'Don't look right empty that way. Needs some decorations.'

'Tom, you're getting bloodthirsty,' Slade smiled. 'No way for a peace officer.'

'I hanker to see some more of the right sort spilled,' the sheriff retorted. 'Get busy!'

'Will do the best I can to oblige,' Slade promised cheerfully. 'How about a little coffee?'

The coffee was soon forthcoming from the stove in the back room. They sipped it mostly in silence. Outside, Sanderson was saluting the sunset with the beginning of its usual after-dark turmoil. Crane gloomed out the window.

'All heck could bust loose and nobody would notice it with all that racket,' he growled.

'Don't be impatient,' Slade reproved laughingly. 'To borrow your favorite remark, just a matter of time,'

'Uh-huh, and I've a notion time is running out for some horned toad,' Crane said.

A little later, Slade glanced out the window and stood up.

'I'm going over to the Branding Pen to meet Mary,' he announced.

'Okay,' Crane nodded. 'See you there later; got a little work to do.'

Shortly after Slade reached the Branding Pen and sat down, the carters began rolling in. A man disengaged himself from one of the groups and approached Slade's table.

'Mr. Slade,' he said, his voice low, 'Miss Merril told me to ask you to come down to the cart-building office.'

'The cart-building office?' Slade repeated.

'That's right, sir.'

'Thank you,' Slade acknowledged. The man nodded and made his way to the bar where he ordered a drink, not mingling with the others. *El Halcón* smiled thinly as he stood up.

'The little slips!' he murmured to himself. 'Always they make them, the little slips!' He sauntered out.

Outside, he quickened his pace to the next corner, where he paused to gaze back the way he had come, to make sure he was not followed, although he did not expect to be.

The cart building, a small shack to accommodate tools and needed materials, with a cubbyhole office, stood in the lower town. Across from the office door was a straggle of chaparral growth, perhaps a half-score of yards distant. Slade circled around the growth to approach it from the rear, worming his way through the brush with his catlike tread, hands on the butts of his Colts.

A few more gliding steps and he saw two men standing in the fringe of the growth, eyes fixed on the open office door outlined in the light of a low-turned lamp. The door he was expected to enter.

He called softly.

'Waiting for somebody, gentlemen?'

With startled exclamations the pair whirled, going for their holsters.

Slade drew and shot with both hands. *Left-right-left-right!* And again!

Then he lowered his smoking guns and peered through the powder smoke at the two motionless forms sprawled on the ground.

Sheathing his Colts, he whipped through the brush, circled again, and reached a street, along which he walked rapidly. The shooting would have been heard and somebody would probably come to investigate. Highly unlikely it would have been heard in the Branding Pen.

Evidently it hadn't, for when he reached the saloon the normal hullabaloo was in progress.

The pseudo-messenger was standing at the bar, gazing expectantly at the swinging doors. When Slade entered, his eyes bulged, his mouth dropped open. Slade walked up to him.

'Fellow,' he said, 'your two friends are

waiting for you, down by the cart building.'

Reading the terrible menace in *El Halcón's* cold eyes, the fellow scuttled out the door like a scared rat.

After glancing around to make sure Mary hadn't yet descended from her room in the Regan House, Slade made his way to the sheriff's office to await developments.

They weren't long in coming. Two highly excited gentlemen rushed in gabbling incoherently.

'Shut up and tell me what you're talking about!' bawled the sheriff.

'Which would be the best trick of the week,' Slade thought.

'Two dead men layin' down by the Merril cart shack,' one stuttered. 'D-dead as d-door nails! Shot to pieces!'

'All right, I'll go down there,' said Crane. 'Come along, Walt.'

Outside, with the gabblers going on ahead, the sheriff said to Slade.

'So! Pulled another one, eh? You're the limit!'

'You hankered for floor decorations,' Slade reminded him. 'I aimed to oblige.'

'Please tell me what did happen?' Crane begged.

Slade told him, in detail. 'They made a few of the little slips their brand seem always prone to make sooner or later,' he concluded. 'First was that fellow going to the bar and not at once mingling with the others. Then there were a couple of things they didn't know about. One, that I am thoroughly familiar with all of Mary's workers and knew at once he wasn't one of them. Another, that I had given Mary strict orders never to remain in the building after the others left, to leave with them, The little slips! Always they make them.'

'Here's hoping the head devil of the bunch makes one,' said the sheriff.

'He may have already made one,' Slade replied grimly.

Crane looked expectant, but *El Halcón* did not amplify his remark.

They reached the cart building and found the two bodies right where he left them.

Quite a crowd had gathered, exclaiming, chattering, conjecturing. Crane stilled the uproar.

'All right, some of you work dodgers pack 'em to my office and we'll give 'em a once-over. Looks like maybe they gunned each other.'

The explanation appeared to be generally accepted. 'May keep some folks guessing, eh?' he muttered to Slade, who paused long enough to extinguish the light in the office. Then they followed the procession, which was constantly augmented by new arrivals.

The bodies were placed on the office floor, and argument and wrangling began as to whether the pair had been seen here, there, or elsewhere, with no agreement. Which was just what Slade expected. He said nothing, but listened. Since he had already formed a fairly good opinion as to who was the head man of the outfit, it was not likely that where or with whom the pair had associated meant much.

Mary Merril and Lerner arrived. The

blue-eyed girl glanced accusingly at Slade but did not remark. Lerner smiled slightly and also held his peace.

Finally Slade nodded to the sheriff, who cleared the room of all except Mary and Lerner, and they proceeded to give the bodies a careful once-over. Their pockets revealed nothing save a rather large amount of money, which caused Crane to observe:

'Part of the express-car haul. Quite a bit of it is gold coin, and I understand a portion of what was taken from the safe was coin.'

Slade nodded and gave attention to the dead men's hands, 'Were never cowhands,' he remarked, 'But I'd say they have handled tools of various sorts. Were very likely associated with the railroads or the oil fields.'

'Which is interesting,' observed Lerner. Slade smiled Mary's dainty black brows drew together slightly.

'You should have plugged that wind spider who brought the word, dead center,' the sheriff growled.

'Figured he could possibly be of more value alive,' Slade explained. 'I'll recognize him if I see him again.'

'Guess you're right,' conceded Crane. He chuckled. 'Seems everybody figures the devils gunned each other. Which is all to the good.'

'Fortunately nobody appeared to note the position of the bodies,' Slade said. 'It was hardly that of two men who gunned each other to death.'

'I never thought of it,' admitted the sheriff. 'But of course you don't miss anything. Well, guess we've done all we can here. Next Doc, the coroner, can take over for his inquest without any witnesses. So how about the Branding Pen and a snort or two?'

'Guess we could do worse,' Slade agreed. 'I'm hungry,' said Mary.

In the Branding Pen the killings were being discussed, but as nobody was aware of the part Slade played in the episode, the sheriff was able to have his snorts, Mary her snack without interruption. After which they decided to call it a night.

12

The carts rolled for Tumble the following morning. Slade rode with them, as did the sheriff, a last-minute decision on his part.

'Deputy Ester can keep an eye on things here,' he said. 'He'll send word if anything cuts loose. Feel it in my bones that the next hand played in the game will be at or around Tumble. Wouldn't you, Walt?'

'Is possible,' Slade conceded. 'Anyhow, we'll try and play your hunch. At least the weather is behaving; it's a beautiful day.'

It was — Texas weather at its best, which was saying plenty. Golden sunshine, a sky of deepest blue, a whisper of breeze that rippled the grassheads in amethyst waves, Birds sang in the thickets. Little animals went about their various affairs. Everywhere peace and amity. Except in the heart of cruel man.

'The hellions are sure after you hot and heavy,' the sheriff remarked to Slade.

'But with no luck, which is all that really counts,' *El Halcón* replied.

'Guess so,' nodded Crane. 'But darned hard on the nerves; that is for people that have any, which don't include you,' Slade laughed, and did not argue the point.

Mary reined Rojo in close to Slade and eyed him contemplatively. 'I believe there's less chance of you getting into trouble out here than in town, thank heaven,' she said.

'Don't you be too sure about it,' the sheriff put in. 'Trouble is just nacherly wherever he is. Look at that hilltop over there; enough brush to hide a coupla dozen owlhoots.'

'Uncle Tom, you take all the joys out of life,' Mary protested. 'Now you've got me watching hilltops.'

But the sheriff's pessimism proved to be unfounded. Without incident, they reached Tumble shortly before dusk. In Branding Pen Two, Mary trotted up to her room to change clothes, Lerner

142

having remained with the carts to see that everything was in order. Slade and Crane sat down at their favorite table hut refrained from ordering much-needed food until the others joined them.

Suddenly the sheriff, staring at the bar, uttered an exclamation. Slade had already noted what excited him. Standing at the bar, conversing, were Bertram Clag, the Ajax Oil representative, and the carting train owner, Haley Welch.

'Now what the devil are those two doing here?' Crane wondered.

'I understand that Tumble is Clag's real headquarters,' Slade replied. 'Perhaps Welch just came for the ride.'

'Darned unlikely, I'd say,' grunted the sheriff. 'They're cooking up something; I'll bet on it.'

Slade thought the sheriff was probably right, but refrained from comment. He was wondering a little himself, but preferred not to speak his thoughts at the moment.

Mary came tripping down the stairs, modishly garbed, and joined them, declaring she was famished. Slade thought her outfit very becoming and told her so, being rewarded with a smile and a dimple.

Lerner entered a few minutes later, the bellowing carters streaming after him. Slade carefully scrutinized each face that passed to make sure there was no more outlaw infiltration. There wasn't. He turned to give a waiter his order and forgot all about the carters for the time being. He noted that Clag and Welch were still talking together at the bar, and put them also out of his mind.

They enjoyed a very pleasant dinner without interruption, after which Mary wanted to dance and Slade obliged for a couple of numbers.

'But you've got something on your mind now,' she said, bright-eyed and rosy after a fast number. 'Please stay out of trouble for one night. You're causing me to grow old before my time, and I'll have enough of a chore hanging onto you staying young.'

'You're doing all right by yourself,' he

reassured her, 'And I really wasn't building up trouble in my mind. I was just thinking that I spend most of my time hanging around saloons) and I wasn't sent here to hang around saloons. One advantage to a prominent saloon, though. Sooner or later, everybody shows up in it.'

'Like the two gentlemen at the bar you've been studying,' she murmured before they reached the table.

'Don't miss much, do you?' he chuckled. 'Did I ever?' she retorted.

'Very seldom,' Slade conceded.

'But of course there's always a first time,' she admitted, adding, 'though I don't think it's this time.'

Their glances met, with understanding.

Lerner had been unusually silent all evening, and Slade knew he had something on his mind. A young carter asked Mary to dance. The sheriff moved to the bar for a few minutes. Slade turned to Lerner.

'All right,' he said, 'let's have it. What's

bothering you?'

'I'm afraid there's trouble in the making,' Lerner replied.

'Yes?'

'Yes. Between the oilmen and the ranchers. You quieted them down the last time you were here, but it looks like the enmity may cut loose afresh.'

'Because of what?' Slade asked.

'Appears a cowhand from Martin Gladdens Lazy G spread was badly beaten by a couple of oil field workers. The other cowboys have sworn vengeance. Already a few shots have been fired over the field. Nobody hurt so far, but by the looks of things, it's just a matter of time until somebody is. The field workers are beginning to arm and vow to retaliate if there is any more shooting. A pretty kettle of fish, and how to get the fish out before they spoil or boil is more than I can figure, excusing an old expression that I feel sorta applies.'

'May be somewhat hackneyed, but I believe it does,' Slade said.

He sat silent for several minutes; he

had just heard some disturbing news. A real rukus between the oil workers and the cowhands could be a very serious matter. There were many oil workers, but the other holdings would quickly combine with the Lazy G to even the odds. A range war of the worst sort in the making, and it was up to him to put a stop to it before it got completely out of hand.

Of course a word to Captain McNelty would send a dozen Rangers into the section to enforce the law and order. But to do so would admit failure on his part to do the chore he had been sent into the section to perform. Such a thing had never happened before, and he grimly made up his mind that it was not going to happen this time. And already he had a pretty good idea of what it was all about, and its purpose.

'What did I tell you!' yelped Lerner, jumping from his chair.

From the direction of the trail that ran past the north edge of the town sounded a volley of shots followed by a storm of yells and curses.

More shots! More yells! The beat of horses' irons on the trail!

'Come on,' Slade said. They went through the swinging doors together.

Spurring west on the trail were half a dozen horsemen, still shooting at the field, fading into the distance of the night. At the edge of the trail was a crowd of oil field workers.

'Here's another blankety-blank-blank cowhand!' bawled a brawny rigger. He rushed at Slade, big fists flailing.

Something like the slim, steely face of a sledge hammer smacked against his jaw like a butcher's cleaver on a side of beef. He turned a flip-flop, landed on his back, stayed there. Slade's great voice rolled in thunder through the tumult:

'Shut up your gabbing! What's the matter with you, have you all gone completely loco? Shut up, I said!'

He got order, or something resembling it. Somebody shouted:

'That's Mr. Slade, the special deputy! Did you see the homed toads, Mr. Slade?

The blankety-blank cowhands!'

'How do you know they were cowhands?' Slade countered.

'Why — they were dressed like cowhands,' replied the other.

'Which is no proof they are cowhands,' Slade said. 'You are dressed like an oil field worker, but how do I know you aren't a cowhand in disguise?'

The sally brought a general laugh — even the man who was the recipient of the jibe laughed — and eased the tension.

'Suppose we find out what damage was done before we do any more talking,' Slade suggested.

Examination proved the damage was minor. A couple of derricks had been peppered with bullets, a walking beam pully knocked from its spindle, the hoisting line fouled. Appeared nobody had been nicked by the flying lead. For which Slade was duly thankful.

'Mr. Slade,' a well owner asked, 'if it wasn't cowhands doing the shooting, who was it?'

'Frankly, I don't know, not for sure,' Slade answered. 'But I intend to find out.'

'He'll find out, all right,' another owner put in, and it'll be just too bad for the gents he's looking for.'

'By the way,' Slade continued, 'I was told that what started the trouble was a cowhand being beaten by a couple of oil workers. How were these oil workers dressed, does anybody know?'

'Why, I guess they were dressed like oil workers,' the owner who had first spoken replied.

'Which does not conclusively prove they *were* oil workers,' Slade pointed out. There were nods as his listeners got the drift of the remark. Slade was satisfied that he had sown seeds of doubt in the minds of the gathering. He figured his next chore was to employ the same procedure on the cowhands.

A brawny rigger with a swollen jaw sidled up to the Ranger.

'Mr. Slade,' he said sheepishly, 'I reckon I made a mistake.'

'You look it!' somebody barked. Laughter!

'Uh-huh, trying to trade punches with *El Halcón* is just like tryin' to trade bullets with him — a plumb losing game,' chuckled the owner. More laughter.

'So don't go jumping at conclusions and going off half cocked,' Slade advised. 'Be seeing you all.'

With Lerner beside him, he returned to the Branding Pen Two, where he found Mary in no very good temper.

'Two more gray hairs for me,' she said accusingly. 'When you dashed out of here I figured you were going to tackle the whole bunch of them singlehanded.'

'Why, I wasn't alone,' he protested. 'Lerner was with me.' Miss Merril sniffed daintily and let it go at that.

'But he sure took over that bunch of oilmen,' said Lerner. 'Now they don't know for sure what to think.'

'I can sympathize with them,' Mary answered. 'I'm always in that category where he's concerned.'

Slade noted that Clag and Welch were

no longer at the bar.

'They left while you were out,' said Mary, interpreting his glance. 'A couple of men dressed like cowhands came in and spoke with Mr. Clag. All four left together. You didn't see them outside?'

Slade shook his head. 'So much excitement and mixing around that I could easily have missed them.'

'That I doubt,' Mary replied. 'More likely they deliberately avoided you.'

'Why?'

Mary shrugged. 'Oh, I don't know,' she said, 'Feminine intuition, perhaps.'

Slade smiled and did not press her to explain. After all he had a lively appreciation of feminine intuition, or instinct. It had proved of service to him before, Lerner who had been an interested listener, nodded emphatic agreement.

Sheriff Crane, who had also hurried out when the shooting started, returned, growling under his mustache.

'Thank Pete you read the riot act to those *loco hombres*,' he said. 'Now if you can just put a flea in a cowhand ear or two, perhaps you'll straighten out this mess.'

'Here's hoping,' Slade said cheerfully.

'Waiter!' barked the sheriff. 'A couple of snorts.'

'Coming up,' replied the waiter. 'Wine for the lady, right? And coffee for Mr. Slade.' He hurried off to fill the orders.

After the sheriff downed his snorts, he glanced at the clock and remarked, 'Well, looks like things have quieted for a spell, so suppose we call it a night.'

'I'm in favor of it,' said Mary. 'Has been a long, hard day, and I've got another one ahead of me.'

There was a general concurrence.

13

The following morning found Mary and Lerner checking the unloading and apportioning the cargo, which was gratefully received by the well owners, who were well pleased and eager for more.

'I'll end up skin and bones because of them,' Mary sighed.

'Well, you're a long way from that now,' said Lerner, eying her proportions with appreciation.

'Getting fat from worry is just as bad,' she complained.

'And that doesn't apply either,' he chuckled with another look that caused her to giggle and blush a little.

Meanwhile, Slade was riding east on the trail that was in existence long before the inception of Tumble, which, after servicing the ranches, joined the east-west trail to Sanderson.

His first stop was the Lazy G casa, where he received a warm greeting from old Martin Gladden, the owner. Over cups of steaming coffee they discussed the situation.

'An old dodge that's been practiced here and elsewhere,' Slade said. 'Get two factions on the prod against each other, giving the outlaws a free hand to operate with little fear of detection or interruption. Yes, an old procedure, but handled properly it works, and the outfit plaguing the section knows how to handle it.'

'Guess you're right,' conceded Gladden. 'You always seem to be. Anyhow, I'm sure glad you showed up. I'm willing to swear that none of my boys, nor any of the other spreads either, have shot up the field, but I was beginning to be afraid we couldn't hold them in much longer. One of mine got an awful beating in town by two devils; was bad sick for several days. Something more like that and the roof will cave in.'

'I'm confident the two responsible were not oil field workers,' Slade told him. 'They pretended to be, of course, with the express purpose of stirring up trouble between the oilmen and the ranchers.'

'Guess you're right again,' admitted Gladden. 'I'll help spread the word around that *El Halcón* is on the job and to do as he says.'

Slade visited the other ranch houses with similar results. As he beaded for town through the glory of the sunset, he felt he had accomplished quite a good deal. He had managed to instill doubt in the minds of the cowmen, too. Let the leaven work a while and see what it brings forth.

It was long past full dark when he reached Tumble to find Mary and the sheriff awaiting him.

'What, no carcasses?' said Crane, after he had briefly reviewed the results of his ride. 'You're slippin'.'

'Please, Uncle Tom, don't rush him,' Mary begged. 'He'll be mixed up in something soon enough. It's refreshing to know he just took a peaceful ride.'

'Office floor will be needing decorations,' the sheriff persisted.

'Just give him time,' she repeated.

Miss Merril was to prove herself a prophetess with honor in her own land.

Lerner arrived and joined them. 'All set to roll tomorrow,' he announced. 'Money's safe in Branding Pen Two's strong box. Now I can relax for a while.'

'And I think Walt is due for something to eat,' said Mary. 'How about it?'

'Guess I can stand a snack,' Slade admitted. 'I didn't take time to eat at the various ranch *casas*; was anxious to get back to town.' Mary beckoned a waiter.

Now Tumble's riotous night life was in full swing, the streets crowded, the saloons packed, with everybody apparently endeavoring to outdo his neighbor in making a racket. In Branding Pen Two the din was deafening, the air thick with smoke.

Slade finished his snack, rolled a cigarette. For a while he smoked in silence, studying the crowded room, and noting nothing he considered of importance. Mary and Lerner were dancing, the sheriff wandering about, speaking with acquaintances. Abruptly Slade got to his feet. A breath of fresh air wouldn't go bad, with a little of something other than tobacco smoke to breathe. Mary saw him depart, and her eyes followed him anxiously as he passed through the swinging doors.

Outside was quite a bit better despite the jostling, chattering crowd that thronged the streets. For a while he wandered about aimlessly, studying faces, listening to scraps of conversation, as was his wont.

Gradually he worked his way to the oil fields. Here the cheerful clank and jangle and thud of machinery was a refreshing change from the constant babble of human voices. He strolled around the edge of the field, instinctively keeping in the shadow as much as possible; anything could happen on such a night.

A short distance west of the field was a long and not very high ridge, its crest clothed with thick and tall chaparral growth. Slade scanned the bristle of brush crowning the ridge and extending down the slope almost to its foot. He scanned it with the eyes of *El Halcón*, for he had had experience with that ridge. It was conveniently situated for anybody with designs of some sort on the field. Not far from its foot were two big producing wells that were anchored down for the night.

Suddenly *El Halcón* tensed, staring. Stealthing from the growth and toward the wells were three men, one bearing a bundle of something. Slade's voice rang out:

'Hold it! What are you up to?'

A clatter of exclamations, a whirling toward the sound of his voice, a grabbing for holsters.

Slade took no chances. He drew and shot with both hands. Answering slugs blazed toward him. Ducking, dodging, weaving, he shot again, and again, and to all appearances, as he had done once before, he blew up the world!

A thundering roar, a fluff of yellowish light, a cloud of smoke! Slade was knocked off his feet by the concussion blast of the exploding dynamite.

Dazed, bewildered, he scrambled

erect, staring at the hole blown in the ground. Beside it lay two motionless forms, and what was left of a third, which wasn't much.

Save for the monotonous jigging of the walking beams, all activities on the field had ceased. Men were running toward the scene of the explosion, yelling, cursing. One instantly recognized *El Halcón*.

'What was it, Mr. Slade?' he shouted.

'An object lesson,' Slade replied as he ejected the spent shells from his Colts and replaced them with fresh cartridges.

'A-a-a-what?' stuttered the oilman.

'The lesson,' Slade explained, 'is Don't go in for a gunning session while you're packing a bundle of dynamite. The sort of messed-up gent over there by the hole learned it too late to do him any good.'

'He sure looks it,' was a voice of agreement. 'What was he going to do with the dynamite?'

'Blow those two wells, and cave in the bores, an expensive repair chore for the owners,' Slade explained. A volley of cuss words followed.

Sheriff Crane puffed up, with him Lerner and Mary Merril.

'Well, there are the floor decorations for which you hankered,' Slade told him. 'Only one will need to be covered; he doesn't look very nice undraped.'

Mary shuddered. The sheriff spouted some weird profanity, ably abetted by the oilmen. Slade explained how the dismembered gentleman got that way. More shudders and more profanity.

'Okay,' growled Crane. 'Pack 'em to the office and lay 'em out on the floor.'

A large tarpaulin was procured to accommodate the remains of the gent who had carried the dynamite, the other two placed on planks, and the grisly procession go under way.

'Well, didn't I predict it?' Mary said.

'You sure did,' Slade concurred. 'You hit the nail squarely on the head. Get along with some more predictions.'

'I won't,' she declared. 'They might come true.'

In the office, after giving the bodies a quick once-over, Slade turned to the assembled oilmen.

'Any of you familiar with range riding?' he asked.

'Got my start following a cow's tail,' one confessed.

'Take a look at this pair's hands,' Slade said. The oilman did so.

'Were they ever cowboys?' Slade asked. The oilman shook his head.

'Never were,' he said. 'Not the slightest indications of rope and branding-iron scars. Nope, they never were.'

The oilmen glanced at each other, nodded their understanding.

'But Mr. Slade, if the hellions ain't cow hands and never have been, who are they and why have they been doing the things they have?' was a question.

'I'll repeat what I said last night,' Slade replied. 'I don't know, but I intend to find out.' More nods.

'He'll find out, all right,' declared the sheriff. 'Ain't no doubt in my mind as to that.'

'Guess he will, and it'll be just too bad for the devils when he does get a line on 'em,' said an oilman. 'He sure took care of those three proper.'

'Well, 'pears nobody remembers seeing the blasted wind spiders before,' said Crane. 'So I reckon we might as well close up shop. Doc Cooper, the coroner, can take over from here on, How about Branding Pen Two? I crave a snort.'

To which nobody objected. The sheriff shooed everybody out and locked the door.

As they sat down at their table in Branding Pen Two, Mary remarked, 'There's Mr. Clag at the bar; he looks to be in a bad temper. Perhaps he has reason to be.'

'It is possible,' Slade conceded. He had already noted that this time the gleam in Clag's eyes was not one of amusement. Rather, it was one of baffled anger. Slade smiled slightly and rolled a cigarette.

Mary glanced at the clock.

14

The carts rolled the following morning. Slade rode with them, the money received for the preceding day's unloading stashed in his saddle pouch. He had arrived at the conclusion that the outlaws would resume operations around Sanderson, having had no luck in the Tumble area.

Sheriff Crane also rode, saying that it was time he got back to where he belonged. Slade's resolve to accompany the carts was strengthened by the sheriff recalling that the next day was payday for the railroaders and the cowhands of the neighboring spreads. Paydays sometimes provide opportunity for an owlhoot bunch.

'Here's hoping it'll be a peaceful one for a change,' said Mary. 'We could sure use one of that sort.'

The sheriff shook his head. 'Nope, won't do,' he replied. 'My Sanderson office floor needs some decorations.'

'Uncle Tom, you're becoming blood-thirsty as a Comanche,' Mary reproved.

'Like to see the proper sort shed,' admitted Crane. 'Keeps the right kind of people from losing any.'

'Guess you have something there,' the girl agreed.

'The carts rolled on through the warm glow of the sunshine, for the nice weather prevailed, with promise of several more days of the same. Twigs and branches were frescoed with gold, and the grass-heads were developing a touch of amber.

It was good to be alive on such a day, Slade thought, and everything consid-ered, he was fairly well satisfied with what he had accomplished in the course of his sojourn in the oil town. Now if the luck would just hold a little longer, there was a chance that in Sanderson he might get an opportunity to dean up the whole mess once and for all. He rode on beside Mary, his mind at ease.

For now he had no doubt as to who was the head of the owlhoot outfit and would be able to concentrate on him instead of being forced to spread his attention over several possible suspects. Which made quite a difference.

The carts reached Sanderson shortly before sundown and were at once placed in loading position, because the Tumble oilmen were yelping for casings and other badly needed materials.

'I don't know how long I can take this without going plumb loco,' Mary sighed to Slade. 'But I pledged my word and I reckon I'll have to make good.'

'Yes, looks like you haven't much choice,' Slade conceded. 'And now — '

'And now I'm going over to my room and clean up a little,' she said. 'See you in the Branding Pen for dinner.'

Slade enjoyed a sluice in the icy waters of the trough in the back of Shadow's stable and, as always, was greatly refreshed thereby. He went out and strolled around a bit.

An air of expectancy hovered over Sanderson. Payday was always an event for the Border town, and the prevailing fine weather presaged an unusually lively one. Slade looked forward to it with anticipation, for he experienced a premonition that he might well be able to do some business before it was over. He dropped in at the Hog Waller Saloon for a word with Cruikshanks, the portly owner, paused to gaze at the activities of the railroad yards, and from there made his way to the Branding Pen.

He found Mary, the sheriff, and Lerner already there, waiting to be served.

'And waiting for you we'd starve,' Mary complained, moving her chair closer to Slade's.

'Take it easy,' counseled the sheriff. 'The cook has his orders and is stirring his stumps; Hardrock's in the kitchen with him. You'll eat.'

Lerner nodded toward the bar. 'See our *amigo* Clag, the oil representative, also rode up,' he remarked. Slade had already noted the fact. He did not comment. Mary shot him a quick glance but also held her peace.

'Doc Cooper hankers to hold an

inquest on those carcasses we packed to town with us in about an hour,' the sheriff remarked to Slade. 'Guess you'd better be there, seeing as nobody but you were around when they got their come-uppance.'

The dinner arrived, and all conceded it was worth waiting for and proceeded to do it full justice. After a snort and a smoke, Crane glanced at the clock.

'Guess we'd better amble over to the office, Walt,' he said. 'Doc will be ready to do business in a little while. Get that over with. Sure won't be any chance tomorrow, if we put it off. Couldn't be able to get a jury together sober enough to pass judgment.'

'Okay,' Slade replied. 'Let's go.'

'And perhaps you can stay out of trouble there and back,' Mary hoped.

The inquest was brief. Slade was commended for doing a good job on the hellions and was advised to bring some more of the same brand, in the same shape, as quickly as possible.

The jury and the coroner filed out;

Deputy Ester accompanied them. The undertaker took over. Crane drew the blind and locked the door. He and Slade sat down with coffee and smokes for a short period of relaxation.

'How about doing a little talking?' Crane suggested. 'Ready to tell me who you've got in mind as head of the pack?'

'Yes, I think I am,' Slade answered. 'And I also think you are going to be surprised, although there is little doubt but that Lerner is convinced. And so is Mary, of course. She reads me like a book; just let me glance at somebody and she knows at once what is in my mind. The head of the owlboot oufit is — Bertram Clag!'

★   ★   ★

The sheriff stared. 'Bertram Clag!' he sputtered. 'Never gave him a thought, except a little recently, since he began associating with Haley Welch. I've had an eye on that jigger for quite a spell, wondering a mite about him. He seems to be mixed up in so many businesses 'sides carting and rides about alone so much. Bertram Clag! If that don't take the hide off the barn door! How'd you come to figure it?'

'To begin with, the old tried-and-true process of elimination,' Slade replied. 'I had to single out somebody who would fit into the picture. Somebody familiar with railroading, the oil business, the handling of explosives, and the opening of safes. I studied everybody I contacted, making it my business to contact just about every newcomer in the section who was outstanding in any way. Gradually I discarded my contacts until I had narrowed down to Welch and Clag. To Clag, rather, for I never really seriously considered Welch. He just didn't fit into the picture, despite the fact that some of his habits were peculiar. He's just ambitious, a worker, and trying to get ahead. Whereas Clag did fit.

'In other words, he was a potential suspect, although there was certainly nothing definite against him. But because he was a potential suspect, I began studying him carefully and noticing little things I otherwise would have passed up. I got a couple of looks at the bearded man who appeared to be giving the orders in the course of an outlaw raid. His rather unusual build and carriage, things hard to disguise, were strikingly similar to Clag's. I certainly could not have identified him as Clag, but I was impressed by the similarity. Then there was Clag's rather surprising and apparently unwarranted interest in myself and my activities.

'Also, he's not too good at controlling his facial expressions, especially those of his eyes. Right after he pulled that successful express-car robbery and knocked off a couple of thousand, he regarded me with undisguised amusement. But when I thwarted his attempt to blow the oil wells, his expression when I saw him in the Branding Pen shortly afterward was distinctly other than one of amusement. And his position as an oil company representative and his standing in the community enable him to learn things not put out for general consumption, such as the money stashed in that loaded express car which was to be coupled onto the El Paso Flyer. Little things, yes, but when you add them up they begin to loom big.

'Of course, what clinches the case against him, so far as I am concerned, was Lerner telling me he represented the Ajax Oil Corporation, a subsidiary of the Neches Waterway Company, the outfit I had trouble with at Laredo and Beaumont, whose understanding of ethics is questionable, to put it mildly.'

'Think they're backing him in this deal?' the sheriff interpolated. Slade shook his head.

'I don't think so. After I larruped them in Beaumont for trying to steal the rice farmers' land, they pulled back across the Sabine River into Louisiana. Heard they were operating over to the east. I'm of the opinion they had all of Texas they want. No, Clag is going it on his own, as his brand always does sooner or later.

'Well, there are a few more things I could mention, but I'd say what I've outlined will give you a general idea of why I look sideways at the gentleman.'

'You sure make out a case against him,' Crane nodded.

'Just one thing wrong with it,' Slade replied.

What's that?'

'It wouldn't stand up in court. No bill, the grand jury would say.'

'Got to get the hellion dead to rights, eh?'

'That's my opinion,' Slade answered. 'And it's liable to be quite a chore; he's a smooth article.'

'We'll get him,' the sheriff said cheerfully. 'As I've said about such things before, just a matter of time. Well, I reckon we'd better amble back to the Branding Pen before your little gal begins to wonder. I'm afraid she figures you're not safe in my company. She says I'm as bad as you are when it comes to getting mixed up in rukuses.'

They found Mary not too perturbed,

Lerner and Hardrock keeping her company. The place was unusually quiet for the Branding Pen. Which was not surprising however, with payday just around the corner. So everybody called it an early night.

15

Payday! Payday in a Border town. Although not yet midmorning, the saloons, halls, and stores were all set and waiting. Waiting to reap the golden harvest. The paycar had rolled in on time and the railroaders were lining up to receive their envelopes, which contained a fat bonus for outstanding work on the expanding yards. Cowboys from the nearer spreads were already arriving, racing their horses along the streets, jovially sworn at by skipping pedestrians. Payday! When anything went, so long as toes were not tromped on too heavily. And anything was liable to happen. Which gave Walt Slade, Sheriff Crane, his deputies, and his specials concern.

'I got a feeling in my bones that we're in for trouble,' Crane declared. 'What do you think, Walt?'

'I fear you may be right,' Slade replied. 'The big questions are Where, When, and What. Guess it's up to us to analyze the situation as it stands and endeavor to do a little anticipating.'

'So darn many things,' grumbled the sheriff. 'All the rumholes will be loaded, but they'll be taking extra precautions. There will be a lot of money in the pay-car when it leaves here for Marathon, Alpine and El Paso. Then there's the bank, of course. Doesn't look like they'd make a try for that, but I guess you never can tell, with the sort of hellions we are up against. By the way, I saw that blasted Clag in the Branding Pen when I ate breakfast there. Seemed to me he looked sorta smug.'

'Well try and keep an eye on him,' Slade said. 'I told Deputy Ester to keep tabs on him as much as possible. Ester's a good man and not the sort that attracts much attention in a crowd. I feel he'll handle the chore well.'

'Yep. Bert's a good man, all right, and knows his way around,' Crane agreed. 'We can depend on him.'

'Mary's also keeping watch, and she's

a smart little number,' Slade added.

'She's all of that,' Crane agreed. 'Do you figure he realizes we suspect him?'

Slade shook his head. 'In my opinion, he doesn't. I believe he considers himself too shrewd to have directed suspicion to himself. That's an owlhoot characteristic, and a weakness. I'd say he feels he has definitely kept in the clear.'

'He had until you showed,' grunted Crane. 'I never gave him a thought, and I don't believe anybody else did.'

'Nor did I, for quite a while,' Slade admitted.

'But when you finally did, you did it right,' Crane said. 'By the way, why'd he try to blow up those two oil wells?'

'To intensify the ill feeling between the oilmen and the ranchers,' Slade explained. 'He didn't know I'd talked with both the oilmen and the spread owners and straightened them out. He found out later; that's why he was in such a bad temper when we saw him in Branding Pen Two. His plans in that direction had been knocked galleywest.'

'Just like he'll be when you get through with him,' the sheriff predicted confidently.

'But meanwhile he's very much on the loose, and we'll be hearing from him soon,' Slade said. 'Well, I'm going out and amble around a bit. Meet you at the Branding Pen later.'

Now the streets were crowded. Slade wormed his way through the noisy throng, enjoying the gaiety and excitement. He dropped into quite a few places and found them all booming. Finally he made his way to the railroad yards for a chat with the yardmaster, an old *amigo*.

They talked over past experiences for a while, then Slade asked, 'Bern, what's the paycar's schedule? I understand it is not going to remain here overnight.'

'Well, let's see,' the yardmaster replied. 'It will pull out of here at eight o'clock, make the run to Marathon, do a little paying off there and lay overnight in Marathon and tomorrow continue to Alpine and El Paso, where it has plenty of paying off to do. Why'd you ask?'

'Oh, just idle curiosity, in a way,' Slade answered. 'Sort of like to keep tabs on anything packing considerable money; you know what conditions have been hereabouts of late.'

'I know they have improved quite a bit of late,' said the yardmaster. 'A little more of that sort of improvement and maybe we can relax a bit and enjoy a little peace and quiet for a change.'

Slade smiled at the implied compliment and changed the subject. A little more desultory gabbing and he returned to the sheriff's office, accepted a cup of coffee, and rolled a cigarette, which he smoked slowly, gazing thoughtfully out the window while the sheriff busied himself with some papers.

Abruptly the door was shoved open and Deputy Bert Ester entered, looking excited.

'Maybe it don't mean anything, but I figured that then again it might,' he said. 'I managed to keep an eye on that homed toad, like you told me to. About half an hour ago he rode out of town, rode west on the trail, sorta fast but not too fast. I watched him out of sight. Didn't turn off, just kept riding west.'

'Alone?' Slade asked.

'That's right. By himself, nobody with him.'

For several moments Slade sat silent, the sheriff and the deputy watching him.

'Tom,' he said at last, 'would you like to play a loco hunch?'

'Your hunches ain't loco,' the sheriff said. Ester rumbled sturdy agreement.

'Okay, then we'll take a little ride,' Slade said. 'Round up one of your specials, one that is dependable and can shoot. With him plus you and Bert should be enough to take care of anything we might run into.'

'Old Alf — you remember him — will be just the jigger,' answered Crane. 'Bert, go out and round him up. Find him at the Hog Waller, the chances are,' he told the deputy, who at once slid out the door.

In short order the deputy returned with the special, an elderly, keen-eyed individual Slade remembered well and respected. He, like the sheriff, deplored the conditions payday gave birth to, but, again like the sheriff, there was a gleam in the keen eyes that belied his protestations.

'Okay,' Slade said. 'Lock up and let's head for the stable. Manuel, the keeper, will rustle a cayuse for Alf.'

Pushing their way through the turbulent throng, they gained the stable without incident and quickly cinched up. Another ten minutes and they were riding west on the trail at a fair pace that Slade steadily increased, although not too much, for the horses had a long drag ahead of them.

While making preparations for the ride, Slade's companions had been silent. Now Crane asked a question:

'Just what is your hunch, Walt?'

'That Clag will make a try for the pay-car money after it arrives at Marathon.'

'Alone?'

Slade shook his head. 'He'll pick up some of his bunch on the way. The setup is perfect for them, the car loaded with money for El Paso and laying over the night at Marathon. He couldn't ask for a better opportunity. This schedule has been maintained, or approximated, for years, and nothing like what Clag is planning has ever happened in or around Marathon. But that doesn't mean it can't or won't happen. Some folks who have been lulled into a state of false security stand a good chance of getting an unpleasant surprise. Especially if we slip up on what we are planning.'

'How do you figure the hellion plans to work it?' Crane asked.

'Frankly I don't know and I wish I did,' Slade replied. 'I have an uneasy premonition that it will be something novel and unexpected. We just have to be prepared for anything and, when the time comes, govern ourselves in accordance with developments. Well, we'll see.'

'We'll work 'em, all right,' was the blithe rejoinder. 'We're depending on you and know you won't let us down.

'As I've said before, thanks for your

confidence,' Slade smiled.

The miles rolled back under the horses' speeding irons, the sun dropped down the long slant of the western sky, and the hush of evening brooded over the wild wastelands. The towering mountains seemed to draw nearer, shouldering away the flecks of cloud that were beginning to be splashed with color. Slade grew more watchful, meanwhile racking his brains in an effort to divine just what the shrewd and elusive Clag might have in mind.

Yes, there was no doubt but that it would be something very much out of the ordinary. Well, he had gone up against similar situations and had always made out. He shrugged his shoulders, relaxed a little in the saddle, but did not abate his vigilance. Had Clag by any chance suspected he would meet with opposition, he might be planning a neat surprise for the unsuspecting posse, although Slade was inclined to doubt it. However, he resolved not to gamble on the possibility. Better safe than sorry. Nothing of the terrain over which they were passing escaped his vigilance, and the eyes that probed thicket and hill crest were the eyes of *El Halcón*.

The night closed down, a night brilliant with stars and with a slice of moon in the west making the scene almost as bright as day.

Now Marathon was not too far off, a small community but a bustling one, servicing as it did the vast ranching country of Brewster County, the six thousand square miles of which was as large an area as the combined area of a couple of eastern states. Brewster, incidentally, being but one of two hundred and fifty-four Texas counties!

Slade's vigilance increased, for with Marathon but a few miles ahead, he felt they were on dangerous ground. The trail now ran through a long stand of chaparral with the railroad on the left and at a slightly lower elevation. Through rifts in the growth, Slade could see the rails flowing on and on into the west, on them no obstruction. If there were, the engineer would have plenty of time to halt his train. Looked like nothing would be attempted this side of Marathon. Just the same, *El Halcón* remained very much on the alert; no relaxing with such a character as Bertram Clag on the job.

They had covered another mile and a little more when, faint with distance, sounded a mellow whistle note; the pay-car train was on the rail! Slade moved the posse closer to the growth against the chance somebody in the caboose coupled to the car would observe the little troop and perhaps mention that fact in Marathon, to be overheard by the wrong pair of ears.

On came the train, swiftly overhauling the speeding horses. The boom of the exhaust and the rumble of the wheels reached Slade's ears, quickly loudening. And on and on stretched the shining rails. Now the train was but a few hundred yards behind where the posse rode. Appeared everything was under control.

Then abruptly the whole picture

changed, definitely for the worse. Perhaps a hundred yards ahead of the posse, the top of a tall tree growing close to the right-of-way swayed back and forth violently. To the north it swayed, to the south, back to the north, to the south again, and kept on going until the big trunk thudded across the rails, directly in front of the speeding paycar train.

The booming exhaust snapped off, brake rigging jangled, the brakes ground against the tires. Over went the reverse bar to the rear of the quadrant, the exhaust bellowed, the tall drivers, spinning in reverse, shaved off ribbons of steel from the rails and threw out showers of sparks.

With brake, bar, and throttle, the engineer tried frantically to save his train.

To no avail! Its speed little reduced, the locomotive hit the big tree trunk and spun it through the air. The engine flipped over half on its side to the accompaniment of steam roaring from broken pipes. The front wheels of the splintered paycar left the iron, but the rear wheels stayed on the rails, as did the caboose.

From the growth bulged six men, shooting at the engine and the caboose, making a rush for the rear steps of the paycar.

'Let them have it!' Slade roared as he sent Shadow crashing through the brush to the right-of-way.

He reached it, jerked the horse to a slithering halt, both guns blazing. Beside him were the posse members, firing as fast as they could pull trigger.

A thin rack dimmed the moonlight; steam and smoke from the wrecked engine billowed and rolled in clouds. It was almost blind shooting, but a wrecker fell at the posse's first volley. Slade shot with both hands and another went down. Slade tried to spot the bearded outlaw but could not. A slug grazed his forehead, the shock throwing him off balance for an instant. Through the bell notes ringing in his ears, he heard a crashing in the growth, followed by a thud of hoofs on the trail. He knew it was the bearded man making good his escape, leaving his companions to fight it out.

Which they did, with no thought of surrendering. Back and forth gushed the lances of flame. Slade heard a gasping curse beside him and knew one of the posse had stopped one. Recovering his balance, he shot again and again, at targets that were barely visible, shifting, weaving in the murk. Bullets hissed past him, one ripping the sleeve of his shirt, another just touching his thigh. His companions' guns were booming an echo to the bellowing of his Colts. The hammers clicked on empty shells. He reloaded with frantic speed, tried to line sights with a shadowy form that abruptly vanished, suddenly realized there was no more lead coming his way, only silence.

'Hold it!' he shouted. 'I'm sure they're all down.'

They were. On the ground lay five of the wreckers, shot to pieces.

16

'Wasn't somebody hit?' Slade asked anxiously. He was relieved to learn that a slight bullet furrow across Alf's left arm was the only casualty.

'Surprise worked well for us,' observed the sheriff. 'Guess they didn't know what hit them. They seemed to just shoot without aiming at all. And from the way they're cussing, I'd say the train boys ain't damaged much.'

'I'll take care of everybody shortly,' Slade said. 'Bert, you hightail to Marathon and locate Sheriff Chet Traynor and have him ride over here and take charge of things; we're in Brewster County, you know. Go ahead, only a couple of miles. Traynor will call Sanderson and tell them to send the wreck train to clean up this mess.'

The engineer and fireman had clambered out of their iron cayuse with little more than bruises and a slight cut or two, the same applying to the train crew. The paymaster, who had been snoozing on a bunk, had suffered no injury. A little salve and a couple of pads from Slade's saddle pouch took care of the minor hurts.

'But if it wasn't for you fellers, I've a notion we would all have got bad hurt,' declared the paymaster. 'A killer bunch or I never saw one.' Slade was inclined to agree.

'Saved the money in the safe, and it's plenty,' added the paymaster.

'You can count on Mr. Slade always being right where he's needed,' chuckled the conductor, rubbing his bruised noggin.

The brakemen chortled agreement as they hurried east and west to flag down all traffic. Slade changed the subject by suggesting the outlaw horses, doubtless tethered in the brush, be located for Sheriff Traynor to pick up. Which was done.

With lanterns and torches going, now there was plenty of light, by which

Slade and Sheriff Crane examined the dead outlaws, hard-looking specimens with nothing outstanding about them so far as Slade could ascertain. They were pretty well masked by neckerchiefs tied up high.

'But Clag wore none,' Slade commented. 'Wanted to be seen, if he was spotted by somebody, wearing a beard.'

'You feel sure it was him got in the clear?'

'Of course,' Slade replied. 'Got a break, per usual. A slug had knocked me dizzy for a moment, and by the time I got my brains unscrambled he was into the brush, on his horse, and gone. Oh well, maybe his luck will run out some time.'

Bluff old Sheriff Traynor arrived shortly. 'See everything is under control, just as I figured it would be,' he said as he shook hands with Slade. 'I wired Sanderson, and the wreck train is on the way. A light wagon following me, bringing reliefs for the paymaster and the train crew. Will roll them to their quarters in Marathon. We'll pack the carcasses, too, and the paycar money, just in case. They'll have that car loaded with railroad police when it rolls west. Putting up the corral bars after the cayuses have vamoosed, but that's the way things are done. Restaurant across from my diggin's is all set to look after you fellers, with a stable around the corner for your nags.'

'We'll give them a few hours' rest and then back to Sanderson,' Slade decided, 'We may be needed there. If you want us for an inquest, send a wire.'

'Paymaster and train crew will be all the witnesses we need, if we decide to hold one,' Traynor replied. 'just a waste of time. Say, how'd they manage to drop that tree across the tracks right in front of the train?'

'Simple, effective, and original,' Slade explained. 'Secured a long and strong rope to the trunk, high up. Sawed the trunk nearly through with a prop to keep the tree from being blown over by the wind. When they heard the whistle, they kicked out the prop. A couple of hard pulls on the rope and down she came! Typical of the shrewd hellions.'

'They're some punkins, all right,' Traynor agreed. 'Well, here comes my wagon, and you fellers might as well amble; I'll handle the situation here. Everything westbound is being held at Sanderson, eastbound at Marathon, until this mess is cleared up. Be seeing you.'

Half an hour later found the posse comfortably ensconced at the restaurant, with snorts and filled plates in front of them.

Not such a bad night after all, even though the head devil made good his usual escape, Slade thought. His hunch had proven a straight one; they had saved the paycar money and done for five more of the hellions. Not too bad.

He pondered the unusual character he was up against. Music does strange things to people. He hadn't forgotten the tortured look in Clag's eyes the night he, Slade, was singing in the Hog Waller saloon. It was the expression of a man who gazes back into his past and doesn't like what he sees there — lost opportunities, perhaps, thwarted hopes. Yes, the same old story. Once again, an able man with a touch of genius who somewhere, for some reason, had taken the wrong fork in the trail. Not the first such he had encountered, and doubtless not the last.

'Did you figure some of those wind spiders were once cowhands?' the sheriff asked.

'Three had been, two had not,' Slade answered.

'What of the brands on those nags they rode?'

'Slick-ironed burns, mean nothing.'

The sheriff nodded and downed his snort.

They had finished eating and were smoking and talking when Sheriff Traynor rolled in.

'Wreck train on the job,' he announced. 'Will take them quite a while to get that engine and car in shape to travel, but they nearly had the main line cleared when

194

I left. Well, if you've stowed away your surrounding, suppose we amble over to my diggin's where we'll be comfortable with coffee, Okay?'

Nobody objected, and they took advantage of the suggestion.

'Bill's taken care of,' said Traynor. 'You're my guests.'

It was more comfortable in Traynor's 'diggin's,' as he called them, and they relaxed with steaming coffee and smokes.

'And you'd better wash that streak of blood off your noggin,' Crane told the Ranger. 'Your gal is going to be hard enough to get along with as is, with us gallivanting off without a word to anybody. She'll be worse if she thinks your head is busted.'

Although he believed Mary was not going to be too perturbed, Slade did so, making the slight bullet burn hardly noticeable.

They gave the horses a couple more hours to rest and digest their meal, then set out for Sanderson at a moderate pace.

Although it was broad daylight when

they reached the railroad town, the pay-day celebration was still going strong, and apparently would be for some time. The specials reported no serious trouble.

'Thank Pete for that,' growled the sheriff. 'I for one have had enough excitement to hold me for a while.'

Manuel, the stable keeper, promised to take care of the horses, and the weary riders made their way to the Branding Pen, which was doing plenty of business. The carters were there, looking considerably the worse for wear but still merry and noisy.

Mary had taken their unexpected departure philosophically.

'Guess I'm getting used to it,' she said. 'But now that you're back safe, I'm going to bed.'

'A notion,' Slade agreed. 'I'll walk you to the hotel.'

The sheriff chuckled.

★ ★ ★

The returning wreck train brought the full story of the thwarted robbery to Sanderson, and when Slade descended to the street shortly after sunset, the town was buzzing over it.

He at once made his way to the sheriff's office for coffee, to fortify himself against the bombardment he would very probably meet with in the Branding Pen.

'Some folks already been here asking questions,' Crane said as he locked the door. 'I chased 'em out, figuring you'd be here most any minute. Here's a cup, steamin' hot. I'll have one with you. No, I haven't had any breakfast either. Waited to eat with you and help you face the onslaught.

'You can hardly blame people for being worked up,' he added. 'Nothing just like it ever happened before.'

It was an onslaught, all right, but Slade conceded that the interest and curiosity were warranted and gave a brief summary of the incident, the sheriff putting in a word to give credit where he felt credit was due. Finally Hardrock and the Hootmen took over, and the two peace officers gave a waiter their breakfast order.

Mary bounced in, gay and animated, making a face at the sheriff's twinkle and plumping into a chair close to Slade.

'Actually got a little work done,' she announced. 'Some of the boys showed up before dark, and they and Mr. Lerner at once got busy. We'll finish the loading before noon tomorrow and be all set to roll. I'm hungry!'

After they finished eating, Slade and the sheriff smoked and talked, discussing the situation as it stood.

'Anyhow, I've a notion the devil is fit to be hogtied about now,' Crane observed.

'I only hope he's angry enough to do something rash,' Slade said. 'Despite his proven ability, I have him tagged as a passionate, impulsive man who might fly off the handle in a fit of rage. It is when his hot temper has cooled that we must be wary. Well, we'll see.'

'I'd say he's getting sorta short on spending money,' Crane commented.

'Which means he'll be active soon,' Slade replied.

'Think there are many of the devils left?'

'Hard to tell,' Slade said. 'I'm of the opinion that he may still have two or three of his original bunch, the most competent ones, which would be plenty to cause trouble. The replacements he manages to enlist are quite likely of a smaller caliber, but salty hellions, like those who shot it out with us in the course of the paycar raid.'

'Yep, they were plumb rapscallions,' the sheriff agreed. 'Well, they'll learn what real toughness is before you're finished with them. Let us drink!' He raised his glass.

'Here's to catching up with the hellion, pronto,' he toasted. 'Wherever the devil he is.'

'You'll very likely learn where he is and what he's up to,' Slade replied grimly.

As usual, *El Halcón* was right in his prediction.

17

Langtry was a small community but a prosperous one, servicing as it did quite a few little hamlets in the vicinity. Less than a mile distant was Old Langtry, where Judge Roy 'Law West of the Pecos' Bean held court, dispensing justice with a sixshooter handy. The judge's courtroom in his saloon was unusually well behaved.

The story goes that the judge invited Lily 'The Jersey Lily' Langtry, a popular actress, to visit his saloon in the town that wasn't called Langtry in those days, but Vingaroon, a railroad construction camp. She did so, and he renamed the town Langtry in her honor.

Gentlemen of questionable antecedents who did business across the nearby Rio Grande found Langtry to their liking and spent more than a little money in its saloon and other establishments.

The most outstanding building housed

Josh Sidman's General Store, which did plenty of business. The windows were heavily barred with iron, the front and back doors doubly barred. Sidman slept in the building, in a little room off the store.

The citizens of Langtry usually went to bed early. By midnight the town was quiet.

It was a little past midnight when a man emerged from a stand of chaparral in back of the store. He paused a moment to glance around, then stole forward. Looped to his belt was a coil of thin but strong rope.

Near one side of the building grew a tall tree, its stout branches brushing the eaves. Above was a large skylight in the roof. Moving quietly, the man climbed the tree, eased out along a branch until he reached the roof. Still moving in utter silence, he crept up the slanting roof to the skylight, A little work with a tool, a sharp but not loud click, and the skylight was unlocked and opened. The intruder secured the rope to a transverse bar and let it dangle into the store. He wormed his way through the opening and slid down the rope, still without making a sound.

Reaching the floor, he glided to the front of the store and unbarred the front door. Three more men entered, soundlessly, one tall and bearded, the others with neckerchiefs pulled high, hatbrims pulled low. The bearded man gestured to the office, into which his three companions moved. He, evidently perfectly familiar with the layout of the building, slipped back through the store to the door of Sidman's room.

The creak of his opening door awakened Sidman. He raised up, saw by the moonlight streaming through a window a tall, bearded man looming over him. A gun barrel crashed against his skull and he fell back on his bunk, unconscious. The bearded man left the room and joined his companions in the office, where stood a big old iron safe.

There was always money in that safe but, as a rule, not a great deal. Today was an exception. It contained a large sum

Sidman had drawn from the Sanderson bank to pay a contractor who was going to add another wing to the building.

The slide of a bull's-eye lantern was drawn open, the beam directed on the face of the safe. A man knelt in front of it, manipulating a hand drill. Followed a slight rasping sound, as if a rat with metal teeth were gnawing a pipe under the floor.

A second man moved to the front door, which he opened a crack, giving him a view of the street, and stood there, gun in hand.

Hole after overlapping hole was bored around the combination knob. In a surprisingly short time the knob was lifted out, the door swung open, and the safe looted of its money contents, which was dropped into a sack held by the bearded man, who exclaimed soft satisfaction over the size of the sum.

Without a glance toward where the storekeeper lay senseless, the four robbers left the building by way of the front door, closing it behind them. After a quick look in every direction, they walked swiftly around the building and to the chaparral stand. Another moment and the beat of horses' irons sounded, fading westward.

★ ★ ★

Many hours passed and it was almost dawn when Sidman, the store owner, regained consciousness. He sat up and was immediately deathly sick, holding his bloody head in his trembling hands. After a while he summoned enough strength to stagger to the front door and lurch through it, yelling his loudest.

It took considerable more time for him to arouse the somnolent citizens and make them understand what had happened. Then there was a to-do for fair. A messenger was sent speeding to Sanderson to notify Sheriff Crane of the outrage and summon Doc Cooper to care for the injured storekeeper.

Experiencing a premonition that something was going to happen, Slade had joined the sheriff, always an early riser, in the office and was present when the messenger arrived to gabble out his story of the depredation.

However, there was nothing either could do about it, for the time being, at least. All the messenger could tell them was that Sidman had been knocked cold, the safe robbed.

'And you say Josh didn't get a really good look at any of the devils?' Crane asked.

'He said he just got a glimpse of a big hellion with whiskers before he was hit,' replied the messenger. 'We thought you'd oughta know about it.'

'Well, guess we'll have to round up all the big jigger with whiskers we know and try and pick the right one,' said Crane.

'That'll be fine,' applauded the messenger, the sheriff's sarcasm going completely over his head.

'Hightail over to Doc Cooper's place so he can amble to Langtry and give Sidman a once-over,' Crane advised. 'Then go to the Branding Pen and have something to eat and a snort or two, on me.'

'Much obliged, sheriff, I'll do that,' the other replied gratefully. 'Got hustled off without any breakfast and am feeling a bit lank.'

After watching him depart, the sheriff turned to Slade.

'Well, the sidewinder didn't waste any time getting busy,' he remarked. 'You hit the nail on the head again, per usual.'

'One did not need to be a marvel of perspicacity to figure it out,' Slade replied. 'We both knew he'd have to have money in short order after the setbacks he's suffered of late. Expect he'd had it in mind for some time. Sidman had been discussing that building project. It was no secret. Clag saw opportunity, studied the layout, which he could do without causing comment, learned Sidman had drawn the money from the bank, and acted. Yes, he's one slippery customer! Well, I'm going over to the cart station to tell Mary I won't be able to ride to Tumble with her today. We'll be getting more details before the day is out, and I wish to hear them.'

They did. Shortly before nightfall two of Sidman's clerks, plus a heavily armed guard, arrived. They would draw more money from the bank on the morrow. They explained to Slade and the sheriff just how the robbery was consummated.

'Got in by way of the skylight, if that don't beat all!' snorted Crane.

'That skylight was an open invitation for an individual of Clag's acumen,' Slade said. 'He never misses a bet.'

'He'll miss one, his last one, and before long,' declared the sheriff. 'Time's running out for that hellion. Oh well, that one last night didn't happen in my bailiwick, Terrel County, but over in Valverde. They thought I should know about it because they figured the devils very likely headed west.'

'But very much in mine,' Slade pointed out. To which the sheriff was forced to agree.

'A wonder they didn't kill Sidman,' he remarked.

'Another example of Clag's shrewdness,' Slade said. 'Let Sidman get a good look at him wearing his false beard. So everybody is talking whiskers. Well, I've had no breakfast and I suppose the same goes for you. So let's hit up the Branding Pen for a small surrounding.'

'Okay with me,' responded Crane, glancing disapprovingly at his floor minus decorations. 'Might hear something there, never can tell.'

When they reached the saloon the robbery was being discussed by those present. But that was about all, discussion. Which was what Slade expected.

'Yes, evidently the devil still has some of his best men on tap,' he observed. 'The way that chore was handled evinces that. He's still in a position to cause plenty of trouble.'

The night passed quietly, which was not marvelous. Clag would hardly be on the rampage again so soon. But *El Halcón* knew they could expect only a brief respite; soon the hellion would be on the prowl again.

Bertram Clag did not put in an appearance so far as Slade, the sheriff, and

Deputy Ester could ascertain. Which caused *El Halcón* to do some thinking. Around noon he arrived at a decision,

'Tom,' he said, 'I'm riding to Tumble.'

'Okay,' replied Crane. 'Hadn't I better go along?'

'Yes, I think you had,' Slade answered. 'And bring Alf, the old special, if you can locate him.'

'I know where he likely is,' said the sheriff.

He had no difficulty locating Alf, and half an hour later found the three riding for the oil town.

'Another hunch?' Crane asked.

'Just a vague notion of one,' Slade replied. 'I've an idea we may be able to do a little business, especially if Clag isn't in evidence in Tumble.'

The sheriff looked puzzled and shot him an inquiring glance, but for the moment *El Halcón* did not choose to elaborate. The sheriff snorted and faced to the front. Old Alf stifled a grin.

The ride to Tumble was pleasant and uneventful. Well before dark they reached the town and stabled their horses. Alf and the sheriff made for Branding Pen Two, where Slade promised to meet them later. He repaired to the cart building to learn how Mary was making out. She was glad to see him, per usual.

'Had a notion you'd show up today, especially after you didn't manage some way to get mixed up in the Langtry store robbery,' she said.

She had heard a sketchy account of the affair from a cowhand who had ridden down from Sanderson, and demanded details, which Slade supplied to the best of his ability. No, she hadn't seen Bertram Clag, nor had the head bartender at Branding Pen Two.

'I'm sure he hasn't been here for several days,' she said. 'Think you'll be able to ride back to Sanderson tomorrow or the next day? Suppose you'll be gallivanting off somewhere pronto. Suppose you are quite disappointed in not being in on the Langtry rukus and will have to tangle with something to soothe your injured feelings.'

'I'm being maligned,' he declared. 'You know I never go looking for trouble.'

'Oh, of course not. You just stand still and wait, all you have to do. Mr. Lerner will take care of things here so let's drop over to Branding Pen Two. I'm hungry!'

When they had given their orders and were waiting for them to be filled, Slade asked a question. 'Any cow stealing of late, Tom?'

The sheriff shook his head. 'Hasn't been any since you landed in this section; at least nobody has reported any.'

Slade nodded, his eyes thoughtful. Mary watched him, a little pucker between *her* black brows.

'Let's see,' Slade remarked. 'First spread to the east is Bob Kerr's Four K, is it not?'

'That's right,' the sheriff replied.

'And next comes Martin Gladden's Lazy G.'

'Right again.'

'Gladden's is the big one, is it not?' Slade pursued.

'Biggest in the section; runs clear to the river.'

'And with a good ford at its foot.'

'About the best hereabouts.'

Slade was silent for a moment, Mary watching him closely. Then, 'Is the holding patrolled?'

The sheriff shrugged. 'Oh, after a fashion, I reckon,' he conceded. 'Gladden hasn't lost any cows for quite a spell and I wouldn't be surprised if he is a mite careless.'

'I see,' Slade said, and addressed himself to his food, which arrived at that moment. Mary sighed and tackled her own plate. Old Alf, the special, did likewise, minus the sigh.

Without interruption, they enjoyed a leisurely meal. Alf and the sheriff chatted with Mary, but Slade was mostly silent, apparently engrossed by his own thoughts.

Mary topped her dinner with a small glass of wine and announced, 'I'm going to the cart station to learn how Mr. Lerner and the boys are making out.

There was some squabbling among the oilmen as to who would get what. I quieted them down for a while by promising more loads without delay, but they may be at it again. Please try and not leave before I get back.'

'We won't be leaving early, that's sure,' Slade promised. Mary didn't look too happy over the implied prospect, and flounced out, her curly head high.

'So you do figure on leaving later, eh?' remarked the sheriff.

'A couple of hours after dark, round up Deputy Blount and we'll take a little ride east.'

'East?'

'Yes, to Martin Gladden's Lazy G spread.'

'You figure the hellions might make a try for some of Gladden's critters?'

'Somehow I've a feeling they might,' Slade replied. 'You said there had been no widelooping for quite a spell, which might signify one is about in order. Then Clag hasn't been seen either here nor in Sanderson for a couple of days, which means he's on the prowl somewhere, with something in mind. Logical to believe he's been out on the range somewhere, which makes it also logical that he is thinking in terms of cows, a quick money turnover, and despite his good haul from the Langtry store, I figure he still needs money and will be out to get some as quickly as he can. A herd of fat beefs run across to the Mexica buyers would fill the bill nicely.

'Continuing the trend, it is also logical to believe that if he does make a try, it will be for some of Gladden's cattle. All supposition on my part — pure theory, you might say — but somehow I can't help but feel I'm right.'

'I feel that way, too,' said the sheriff. 'And it might be our big chance. Get the hellion out in the open where there's no place to hide, and Shadow and your long-range Winchester will take care of him for sure.'

'That, I fear, is in the nature of wishful thinking,' Slade smiled. 'But anyhow we have nothing to lose but a little sleep, and it looks like it'll be a nice night for a ride. So round up Blount and tell him we'll meet him at Sebastian's stable a couple of hours after dark.'

'I'll do that,' Crane promised. 'Going to mosey up to the office right now. Be seeing you later. I've a notion your gal is going to be sorta put out, but maybe you can make it up to her when we get back.'

Mary took it resignedly, only begging them to be careful and not take unnecessary chances. Her blue eyes brooding, she settled down to wait.

18

Shortly after two hours past full dark the posse rode east under a starry sky, at a fair pace.

'The ford is at the foot of Gladden's east pasture, but I figure we have plenty of time to get there,' Slade explained. 'Highly unlikely anything will happen before past midnight. Logical to believe the devils will wait until they are sure casas and bunkhouses are dark and quiet, with everybody asleep. If Gladden happens to be properly patrolling his south pastures, it's doubtful if a try will be made. But I'm of the opinion that he is not, giving the possible wideloopers a free hand. Well, we'll find out.'

They rode on, watchful, although Slade felt they had little to fear of an ambush along the way. That would be out of order for even the shrewd Clag. Looked like things were due to work out in a satisfactory manner.

'Yep, I've a notion it's going to be showdown,' 'lowed Crane. 'I just got a feeling that way. What do you think Walt?'

'That you are possibly right,' Slade conceded. 'I sure hope so.'

And then the weather gods, always an unpredictable and cantankerous lot, decided to take a hand.

Up from the south rolled a great black cloud, fold on clammy fold, blotting out the stars; accompanying it, low mutters of thunder that steadily loudened, flickers of lightning playing back and forth across its sable breast.

'Better don our slickers,' Slade advised. 'Looks like we are going to catch it.'

'Blast it, yes!' growled the sheriff. 'And right when everything seemed to be going smoothly. 'This is liable to complicate matters.' Slade feared so too.

On and on came the ominous cloud. It reached the zenith, drifted down the long slant of the northern sky. Now the thunder was a shuddering rumble, the lightning playing almost constantly.

Came the wind! A hurricane blast that set the treetops to swaying wildly. And borne on its wings the rain, a torrential downpour that blotted out all things save when the lightning blazed.

'You'll never be able to spot the ford in this!' wailed the sheriff.

However, to that Slade did not agree. He knew well his uncanny instinct for distance and direction would serve him despite the confusing war of the elements.

'Think they'll make the try in this blasted storm?' queried Crane.

'The storm is playing into their hands,' Slade answered. 'Even if there are patrols assigned to the south pastures, they'd be seeking cover.' The sheriff growled a lamenting curse.

On they forged, drenched, blinded by the glare of the lightning, deafened by the incessant boom of the thunder and the bellow of the wind, the disgusted horses snorting their protests. Until Slade finally called a halt.

'Here we are,' he said. 'Ford's just the

other side of this stand of growth. We're close to the opening that runs through the chaparral to the water's edge. Crowd against the brush and take it easy for a while.'

The posse obeyed orders, growling and grumbling. The horses shivered.

Slade himself, making sure his Winchester was free in the saddle boot, sat gazing north. The lightning flamed, and by its glare his unusual eyes saw what he expected to see, a moving shadow that was undoubtedly a herd of cattle being shoved by riders.

Yes, it was the widelooped herd, but not where he had expected to see it. Far to the north, it was farther to the east, diagonaling south by east toward the river. He uttered an exasperated exclamation.

'What's the matter?' asked the sheriff.

'Outsmarted, that's all,' Slade replied bitterly. 'For some reason or other, perhaps deducing we might be holed up here waiting for them, they are not making for this ford but for the one at the foot of Fisher Farrow's Double F to the east of here. If they reach that ford ahead of us and get them started across, the cows will be goners, and very likely the devils too. Be blind shooting in this mess. Let's go; maybe we can make it.'

He sent Shadow forward at racing speed, the others slogging along behind him through the roaring wind and the blinding rain, getting an occasional sight of the moving herd that steadily drew nearer the rampaging Rio Grande.

On they sped, breasting the wind and the rain. By the lightning flares, Slade caught occasional glimpses of the herd bearing down on the ford and with not far to go. He urged Shadow to greater speed, the big horse responding gallantly, drawing away a little from the others, swiftly closing the distance.

Something sang overhead with the crackling, splitting sound that only a high-power rifle bullet can make.

'They've spotted us,' Slade called to the others. 'Hold your fire another moment.' He drew his Winchester from the boot.

Another slug whined overhead, closer, and still another. Slade flung the rifle to his shoulder, tried to line sights with the vague blurs of the wideloopers, of whom he counted four, with only the instant and dazzling flare of the lightning.

The herd was almost to the edge of the growth through which the opening to the ford ran. Almost but not quite, and before the foremost cows reached it the posse was in action, guns blazing. Slade saw one of the raiders fall. He saw, too, a single horseman flash past the herd and into the narrow opening. His voice rang out:

'Trail, Shadow! Trail!'

The tall horse surged forward, but the milling cattle blocked him. He slashed with his teeth, lashed out with his hoofs, lunged, shouldered. But precious minutes were lost before he hurled the tons of bone and beef aside and won through.

At the water's edge Slade jerked him to a halt. The lightning flashed and he had a flickering glimpse of a single rider more than halfway across the river. He flung the Winchester forward, snapped a shot as the lightning flamed. But as the darkness rushed down he saw the rider kept on going.

Another flash, another shot that he was sure did not find its almost invisible mark. A last mocking flicker and he saw the river was empty, no sign of the lone horseman. To relieve his injured feelings more than anything else, he emptied the rifle into the brush on the far side of the stream, for he had no hope of scoring a hit. Bertram Clag's luck still held. Once more the outlaw leader had escaped.

While he had waited for the lightning to reveal his quarry, Slade had been aware, almost subconsciously, of a roaring gun battle going on the other side of the brush, where the posse was shooting it out with the wideloopers. Now the bellow of gunfire had ceased and only sounds coming from beyond the chaparral were the bawling of the cattle and a rumble of excited voices.

'How you doing up there?' he shouted.

'Okay,' answered the sheriff. 'Did for three of the devils, nobody on our side hurt. You okay?'

'Fine, only I didn't have your luck,' Slade called back. 'My hellion got in the clear.' He turned Shadow and rode up the slight slope to the far side of the growth.

The weather gods had apparently concluded they'd done their damndest for one night. The rain ceased falling, the wind lulled, the thunder gobbled away into the north, the serenest calm descended under a sky brilliant with stars that cast a wan, silvery glow over the scene of carnage.

'I figure we didn't do too bad,' remarked Crane. 'Saved Gladden's cows and gave three more devils their comeuppance. 'Not too bad.'

'Yes,' Slade agreed, 'even though the head of a snake is still on the loose and capable of more fanging.'

'You feel sure it was Clag got across the river?'

'Of course. Another example of his hairtrigger thinking. He's the limit!'

'Maybe the buyers over there did for him,' Crane said.

'You can depend on it that when the buyers heard the ruckus cut loose over here they hightailed,' Slade answered. 'Their business is to purchase wet cows, not mix into gunfights. Let's see, now.'

Old Alf, who was good at preparing against possible emergencies, had a bundle of oily waste in his saddle pouch. He struck a match to it, and by the light they gave the dead outlaws a once-over.

The sheriff 'lowed they were mean looking scuts. Rather above the average was Slade's verdict. All three were former cowhands, he said.

'Quite a bit of money in their pockets, some of the Langtry store loot, I reckon,' said the sheriff. 'Not as much as you might expect, though. Reckon the hellion ain't too well heeled yet. He would have been if he'd managed to dispose of the cows, more than a hundred head of prime beef critters.'

The outlaw horses, well-trained beasts, hadn't strayed far and were easily caught.

The bodies were roped across their saddles, the cattle rounded up and, despite their indignant protests, headed for home.

Progress with the awkwardly burdened horses and the tired cattle was slow, and it was past full daylight when the herd was driven onto the Lazy G ranch-house pasture to the accompaniment of plenty of excitement there.

Slade, not in the best of tempers, gave the owner a sound scolding for not patrolling his holding more efficiently, which Gladden took meekly. He was profuse in his gratitude for the saving of his cows and promised better behavior in the future.

The posse ate breakfast with him, gave the horses a surrounding of oats and several hours of rest, and their own clothes a chance to dry before setting out for Tumble, arriving at the oil town well past noon, where there was more excitement.

The bodies were placed on the office floor, the sheriff refusing admittance to anybody for the time being. The horses were cared for, Mary's fears allayed, and everybody went to bed.

19

Quite a bit past sunset Slade awoke in a fairly satisfied mood despite his irritation over the escape of Bertram Clag. That Clag escaped there was no doubt in his mind. All he had to do was ride west to the next ford, cross over to the Texas side, and continue to Tumble, completely in the clear.

But he was forced to agree with the sheriff that they hadn't done too bad. His hunch had proved to be a straight one.

The hunch, the sheriff well knew, was really the result of a careful analysis of the situation, thinking as the outlaws would be supposed to think and acting accordingly. Which was the explanation of all his hunches, so called.

He bathed, shaved, donned a new shirt and overalls he had purchased a few days before, and descended to the saloon, where he found the sheriff ensconced behind a drink, Mary Merril keeping him company.

'Well, did he make it up to you?' the sheriff asked Mary.

'If allowing me to work all day was making it up to me, I suppose he did,' the girl retorted. 'My carts are ready to roll for Sanderson. Would have rolled this afternoon if he hadn't gallivanted off like he did. Now they'll have to wait until tomorrow. Perhaps I can persuade him to ride with me. That would help some.'

Slade didn't commit himself one way or the other, but ordered some coffee, the sheriff another drink to keep him company. Mary relented to the extent of a glass of wine.

'Now let me have the particulars of last night's happenings,' she requested, 'Old Alf was in a little while ago, but I'm sure I didn't get the whole story from him. He's reticent and just said you had a brush with some cow thieves and came out on top, and Uncle Tom refused to talk until you got here. Now perhaps he will.'

The sheriff did, launching into a graphic account of the affair, giving Slade the credit due him.

Rather more than was due, *El Halcón* thought, but he knew it was no use trying to stop old Tom when he got started on that subject. So he sat back resignedly and listened, or appeared to, for his thoughts were elsewhere. A remark Mary made when the sheriff paused brought him back to his immediate surroundings.

'Clag was here earlier in the afternoon,' she said. 'Mr. Welch was with him. They sat at a table and talked. He said they planned to ride to Sanderson but stopped in for a drink and a bite to eat first. He looked tired, and in not too good a mood; now I understand why.'

Slade regarded her, his eyes thoughtful. He was getting a notion why Clag kept contacting Haley Welch. However he did not comment, although Mary shot him an inquiring glance.

The carts rolled the following morning. Slade rode with them. He felt that if

Bertram Clag was in Sanderson, it was a good idea for him, Slade, to be there, too. He pondered Clag's astounding ability to always slide out of the loop when it appeared to be tightening around him. Well, perhaps the law of averages would finally catch up with him.

The sheriff went along, too. Just for the ride, he said, but Slade believed he was imbued by a similar reaction, relative to Clag's presence in Sanderson.

Mary asked no questions, apparently thankful for the favor vouchsafed her.

They made good time and it was a little past mid-afternoon when they arrived at the railroad town. It had been a pleasant ride under a sky washed clean and blue by the rain of the night before.

The carts were placed in position at the station, ready for loading, the horses cared for. The bank was closed, but Slade had no trouble gaining admission and depositing Mary's money, which he had packed to town in his saddle pouch.

Mary repaired to her room in the Regan House to clean up a bit and change. Slade and the sheriff sat in the office, contemplating the blanketed bodies on the floor and talking.

Naturally the conversation centered around the misdoings of *Señor* Clag, with conjecture as to what would be his next nefarious move.

That he would make a move, and soon, both were convinced. He had suffered some setbacks, but Slade believed his ego was so great that he considered himself personally invulnerable, with more than a little on which to base the assumption. The way he consistently defied death or capture was positively uncanny,

The answer, of course, *El Halcón* knew, was his lightning-fast brain that instantly recognized opportunity no matter how small, and as instantly took advantage of it.

The night before had been an example — streaking through the brush to the ford and across the river before the posse, battling his followers and blocked by the milling cattle, could organize an effective pursuit. And Slade gloomily confessed to himself that more of the same was very likely in order.

In fact, he was beginning to believe that never before had he had such a mind pitted against him. Well, time would tell.

'Doc will hold an inquest on those carcasses we packed to town with us, in a couple of hours from now,' Crane remarked. 'Quite a few folks looked the carcasses over, but nobody could recall seeing them before. Funny, don't you think?'

'I'd say they are very likely from New Mexico or east Arizona,' Slade replied. 'The horses they rode have burns that I'm sure are slick-ironed Arizona brands. Looks like Clag has contacts everywhere. Which is not too surprising. His reputation as a successful outlaw leader must have been spread wide.'

'He was one before you showed up,' said the sheriff.

'Guess the later news hasn't gotten around so much yet.'

'Possibly,' Slade conceded. 'And he would need men experienced in range work to handle a big chore of wide-looping. Gladden said they must have cleaned the cows from around at least three waterholes.'

The inquest congratulated the law-enforcement officers for doing an excellent chore, hoping they'd keep up the good work. The undertaker packed the bodies to Sanderson's long-flourishing boot hill. The sheriff eyed the empty floor disapprovingly.

'Those hellions would have done better by themselves to have stayed in Arizona or wherever they came from,' he said, apropos of the recently removed bodies. 'Texas ain't exactly a good stamping ground for their sort nowadays, at least this section ain't. Well, I figure we've at least earned a snort and a bite. What do you say?'

'I'm in favor of it,' Slade agreed, glancing out at the sunset afterglow. 'Been quite a while since breakfast.'

'And I reckon your gal is already at the Branding Pen, complaining she's starved,' the sheriff added. 'Let's go!'

Mary was waiting for them, all right, admitting she was weak from hunger.

The frustrated widelooping was still being discussed, but Hardrock saw to it that they were not disturbed during their meal, after which the sheriff outlined the details of the affair as he saw fit, apportioning credit as he felt it due. Slade had to put up with praise and congratulations until other attractions absorbed the Branding Pen patrons.

The night passed quietly. Slade danced several numbers with Mary, visited the kitchen help, exchanged reminiscences with Hardrock.

Bertram Clag did not put in an appearance. Which caused Slade to wonder, a trifle uneasily, if Clag had finally realized he was suspect and was going to pull in his horns so far as the Sanderson area was concerned.

Which, *El Halcón* knew, would further complicate the task that confronted him.

However, he need not have worried on that score. There would soon be evidence that Clag was *not* pulling in his horns. Far from it.

The following morning, Slade quickly reversed his opinion anent the activities of *Señor* Clag. Deputy Ester reported that he saw the oil company representative ride east by slightly south.

'Heading for Tumble,' Slade immediately told the sheriff. 'Which means we'll ride with Mary's carts, which will pull out shortly after noon. Guess the only thing we can do is trail the hellion, go where he goes, to the best of our ability. I'll frankly admit that I haven't the slightest notion what he may have in mind, so we'll just jog along and hope for the best. Anyhow, Mary will be glad we're riding with her. She was sort of blue this morning at thought of leaving us here.'

'Can't blame her for that,' said Crane. 'Out of her sight and you're into trouble. Always seems to work out that way, for some reason or other.'

'Just coincidence, I'd say,' Slade smiled. The sheriff grunted and didn't argue the point, although it was fairly certain he didn't agree.

Mary was pleased to learn that they would accompany her to Tumble. 'Uncle Tom is right,' she said. 'Keep you in sight and you don't get mixed up in something.'

Slade was instinctively watchful in the course of the ride, for anything unexpected could happen with such a character as Bertram Clag on the loose.

Nothing untoward took place, and the carts rolled into Tumble just a little past sunset. They were placed in unloading position, the horses were cared for, and something to eat was next in order.

When Slade asked him if he had seen Clag in the course of the afternoon, the bartender at Branding Pen Two shook his head.

'Hasn't been in all day,' he said. 'Figured he was in Sanderson. Think he's here?'

'He rode this way, we understand,' Slade replied evasively.

'Oh, if he's in town he's pretty apt to drop in,' nodded the drink juggler. 'Always does when he's here.'

Slade thought it a trifle strange that Clag had not put in an appearance at Branding Pen Two, but he did not comment, and joined the sheriff at their table.

'Mary will be down shortly,' Crane observed. 'Asked us to wait and eat with her, that she wouldn't be long.'

The evening passed pleasantly enough, but Bertram Clag remained one of the missing. Finally, as the night wore on, in desperation, Slade, the sheriff, and Deputy Blount scoured the town and, to employ Crane's expression, didn't see hide or hair of the blankety-blank-blank.

'What the devil does it mean?' demanded the sheriff.

'It means,' Slade replied quietly, 'that we have been neatly outsmarted.'

'Yes?'

'Yes. Clag did not ride to Tumble. Once he was sure he was out of sight and we were headed to Tumble, he circled back to Sanderson and put whatever little plan he had in mind to work.'

'You mean he's finally caught on that he's suspected?'

'Not necessarily,' Slade replied. 'But it is not illogical to believe, recent happenings taken into consideration, that he'll feel a lot better operating with us out of the picture.'

'Are we heading for Sanderson?' the sheriff asked.

Slade shook his head. 'Would do no good,' he answered. 'Anything he had in mind is either already consummated or will be shortly. No, we'll just sit tight until the word of what was done reaches us, which will be soon enough.'

'Well, it's an ill wind that don't blow anybody any good,' Mary slightly misquoted. 'At least it looks like a peaceful night, for which I'm duly thankful.'

She glanced at the clock, lowered her lashes to Slade.

20

Yes, things were quite peaceful in Tumble, but elsewhere they were anything but peaceful. For right then, Bertram Clag and his outlaws were busy men.

Simon Quale, owner of the Triangle Dot spread to the north of old John Webb's big Cross W, was getting a shipping herd together. He already had nearly a hundred held in close herd around a big waterhole.

Quale was a cantankerous individual and, as the saying goes, he was 'set in his ways.' Let him get a notion in his grizzled noggin and it was well nigh impossible to dislodge it.

The Triangle Dot owner did not guard His herd, holding that as widelooped cows would have to pass over John Webb's holding to reach the river, it wasn't necessary, Webb's spread being always well patrolled.

So only a single hand rode herd on

the cows to prevent straying. Overconfidence can be as infectious as any other emotion, so the cowhand on duty by the waterhole took his responsibility lightly. He ambled his horse around the herd at a leisurely pace, especially after midnight, when the cattle had settled down to chew their cuds and doze.

The hand halted his horse near a straggle of brush to roll a cigarette. A sound behind him caused him to turn his head; he looked into the muzzles of three guns, two held by men with neckerchiefs pulled high, hatbrims pulled low, the third by a tall, broad-shouldered, bearded individual.

'Unfork and lie down on your back,' the bearded man ordered. 'Don't try anything if you want to stay alive.'

The shivering cowboy obeyed; there was murder in the bearded man's pale eyes. The bearded man plucked the young fellow's gun from its holster and tossed it aside. The cowhand, sure his last day had come, lay motionless while his wrists and ankles were bound.

The outlaws proceeded to get the cattle on their feet and moving. Straight south they urged the herd.

However, once they were well out of the cowboy's sight, they changed the direction of marching to almost due west.

Although he had not been bound very securely, it took the hand quite some time to free himself of his bonds. He picked up his gun, mounted his horse, and headed for the Triangle Dot ranch house, which was several miles distant. As he neared the *casa*, he emptied his gun into the air and yelled as loud as he could, quickly arousing ranch house and bunkhouse, the occupants spewing out in all stages of undress. To them he gabbled out his story of the widelooping.

'And you say they headed the herd due south?' asked Quale.

'That's right,' the hand replied. 'I managed to crane my head up from the ground and watched them out of sight. They kept right on going south.'

'Then they can't get away with it,'

Quale said decisively. 'Webb's patrols will intercept 'em and gun 'em down. Guess they don't know about those patrols.'

Perce Archibald, the taciturn Triangle Dot range boss, said nothing, but his brows drew together in thought.

'Going to ride down that way, Boss?' one of the hands asked.

'Oh, sure, to bring the cows back,' Quale decided. 'No hurry, we'll have a cup of coffee first; cook's heatin' it up.'

Quite a little more time elapsed before the outfit was ready to ride. Quale set the pace, not too fast.

Finally, with daybreak not far off, they crossed onto Webb's holding and with the edge of the sun peeping over the eastern horizon, reached his south pastures, with a way to the river and a ford not far off.

From a stand of chaparral emerged two riders, rifles at the ready. A third rider loomed into view, also armed. Quale waved his hat and shouted. After a moment's hesitation, the patrols evidently recognized the Triangle Dot bunch, waved reply, and rode to join them.

'See?' said Quale. 'And if we'd been the cow thieves, they wouldn't have ridden from the brush. They would have thrown lead from it. See?'

'Yes, I see,' Archibald answered dryly, 'but I don't see any herd of cows.'

The two groups merged. Questions and answers were flung back and forth.

'Mr. Quale, I got no notion where your cows went, but they for sure never came this way,' one of the patrol men declared.

'Farther east, maybe?' Quale suggested. The patrol man shook his head.

'If they'd showed over to the east, the boys there would have spotted them and we would have heard the shooting,' he replied.

Quale turned to the young cowboy who had brought the word of the widelooping. 'Real sure you didn't have a bottle stashed in your saddle pouch and with a little help from it dreamed up all this?' he said pointedly.

The cowboy nearly choked with indignation. 'If I figured that big ice-eyed hellion who was running things came out of a bottle, I'd never take another drink,' he snorted.

'Boss,' the range boss interjected, 'Porky's description of how those devils looked tallies mighty close to that of the mighty, mighty smart bunch that has been raising hell hereabouts of late, which nobody could make any headway against until Mr. Slade, the special deputy, showed up and began knocking off the devils. They 'pear to be able to do things that nobody expects to be done.'

Quale swore explosively. Followed a period of profitless wrangling, during which the range boss remarked, 'The fact that they wanted him to see the cows head south and report it is why Porky happens to be alive right now. That's why they didn't tie him very tight — so he could wiggle loose after a bit and hightail to the casa. Otherwise they would have done him in.'

The cowboy shuddered. Quale swore

some more.

Meanwhile, the wideloopers had rolled the herd steadily westward until they were opposite the dark mouth of Echo Canyon, close to the western tip of the Cross W, the only near pass through the hills to the east-west trail.

Time was when Echo Canyon did not believe its name. The acoustics of the narrow gorge had been remarkable. The beat of a horse's speeding irons set up a nerve- shattering drumroll that vibrated the ears like the diapason of hammered steel. A gunshot aroused a spiraling thunderclap that soared to the startled sky. A shout evoked a veritable witch's carnival of howls and wails and bellows in every conceivable tone. A laugh was answered by shrieks of fiendish merriment.

Once discovered by Slade, the explanation was quite simple. Back of the cracked and fissured west wall was a cave. Rising from the cave floor, just about bisecting the width of the tunnel, was a very thin wall of rock that soared upward almost to the lofty roof. Not more than four feet wide at the base, it narrowed to a knife edge at its crest, running nearly the length of the canyon.

It was nothing more than an amazingly extended stalagmite, formed by the drift of calcareous water depositing calcium carbonate during untold eons of time. The thin and broken wall was just a gigantic sounding board that vibrated to sounds concentrated by openings in the canyon wall and magnifying them a hundredfold.

In the course of a gun battle in the cave between Walt Slade and the Covelo outlaw bunch, the added vibrations set up by the reports had brought down the thin wall, crushing the outlaws under hundreds of tons of rock and silencing the echoes forever.

The canyon had not been adequately patrolled for a long time, because it was not a good route for wideloopers, the chief disadvantage being the fact that stolen cattle would be forced to traverse the traveled east-west trail for quite some miles, with always present the danger of being detected before reaching a point where they could come to the river and a ford.

However, into the gorge the rustlers drove the protesting cows. It was the dark hours before the dawn when there was a good chance the trail would not be traveled, or at least by not more than one or two riders, to whom the outlaws would pay little mind.

Out of the south mouth of the canyon bulged the herd, the riders shoving them hard. Mile after mile was covered; and as the east was brightening, the cattle were swerved to the right, down a little slope, and forced to take the water at the ford.

Across the Rio Grande to the brush-grown Mexican shore they bawled and splashed. A few more minutes and cows and thieves vanished from sight in the growth.

Bertram Clag had put one over very nicely.

★   ★   ★

It was close to nightfall and the carts were unloaded and ready to roll when word of the rustling reached Slade and the sheriff, in Tumble.

'Si Quale is fit to be hogtied, I gather,' remarked the sheriff. 'Not so much from losing the cows — he can afford it — but from not being able to figure how he lost them. He swears they must have sprouted wings and flew away. Wonder where they did go?'

'The answer is so obvious that of course nobody thought of it,' Slade replied wearily. 'They went through Echo Canyon.'

'Echo Canyon!' repeated Crane.

'Of course,' Slade said.

'But nobody ever rides through that hole anymore,' the sheriff protested. 'Haven't for years. Practically no cows have been run that way since you cleaned up the Covelo bunch there.'

'Exactly,' Slade conceded. 'So Clag, with his usual shrewdness and courage, took a chance on running into something on the east-west trail, shoved them through Echo and east on the trail to the first ford. Fortunate he didn't run into somebody on the trail, I'd say. Otherwise we might have another murder on our hands.'

The sheriff said several things, under his mustache in deference to Mary's presence.

'Well, the blasted wind spider scored one,' he concluded aloud. 'Guess we'll hafta chalk up a trick for his side, consarn! And he must be pretty well heeled for money now. Figure the pair with him on the widelooping chore are all of his bunch he has left?'

'I rather think so,' Slade answered. 'Two of his best that he has likely been holding back; it would be like the way he works.'

'Odds of three to one ain't bad where *El Halcón's* concerned,' the sheriff said cheerfully.

'Thank you,' Slade smiled, 'but I could do with them a little less lopsided.'

'Never mind,' replied the sheriff. 'You always come out on top. What do you think, Mary?'

'I think,' Miss Merril said primly, 'that a little less persiflage and more *constructive* thinking is in order. There won't be any peace until that man is apprehended, one way or another.'

'You've got something there,' Crane admitted. 'And trying to figure what that per— per— whatcha call it means makes me hungry. Suppose we have something to eat?

Nobody objected, so Slade motioned a waiter, who at once hurried to the kitchen.

The meal, an appetizing one of the cook's best, was consumed mostly in silence, all three diners pondering the problem that was Bertram Clag. After a glass of wine Mary wanted to dance. She and Slade did several numbers. Lerner joined them, and after a period of desultory conversation they called it a night.

The carts rolled early the following morning, with everybody io a better mood, induced perhaps by the blue sky and the bright sunshine.

'Let's just forget everything unpleasant and enjoy ourselves for a while,' Mary suggested.

"Take the goods the gods provide thee," Slade quoted smilingly.

"Lovely Thaïs sits beside thee," Mary completed the couplet. 'I'm not Thaïs, but I'll do the best I can.'

Slade thought it highly doubtful that the famed courtesan was any more beautiful than the girl who rode beside him, the blue of the sky in her eyes and the gold of the sun in her heart.

21

The miles slid back, the western sky grew luminous. The smoke smudge that marked the site of Sanderson came into view, and soon the carts rolled into the railroad town.

The carts were placed for loading, the horses cared for. Slade enjoyed the luxury of a sluice in the icy waters of the big trough in the back of the stable, while Mary repaired to her room in the Regan House. The sheriff gave his office a onceover, and he and *El Halcón* made their way to the Branding Pen to relax and wait for Mary.

Standing at the bar conversing with Haley Welch was none other than Bertram Clag.

Welch shouted a greeting, Clag nodded. Slade was sure the mocking gleam was back in the man's eyes.

The sheriff sensed it also. 'The devil is laughing at us again,' he muttered.

'Guess he feels he has reason to, after the one he put over,' Slade said. 'Don't pay him any mind. Let him still think he's in the clear and that we have no reason to suspect him. Let him live in a fool's paradise of his own making. I'm of the opinion that we are very close to a show-down, and we don't want to do anything that might mar it.'

'Will do my best,' growled Crane, 'but it's a tough chore, with me itchin' for a chance to line sights with the sidewinder.'

'If things work out as I hope they will, you'll very likely get it,' Slade replied.

'I'm still wondering what he and Welch have to talk about so much,' Crane muttered.

'I think I know,' Slade answered. 'Not quite sure, but mighty close to it, I believe. Just take it easy and let developments shape their course. I'm of the opinion he's made the big slip we've been hoping for.'

The sheriff rumbled under his mustache and beckoned a waiter as Mary came bouncing through the swinging doors.

Mary was gay and vivacious, her eyes bright, her cheeks rosy. The sheriff regarded her and chuckled.

'See you had a good night's sleep,' he remarked. She made a face at him and demanded food.

Business was picking up in the Branding Pen, the carters having roared in, reinforced by some of Welch's bunch. There were also cowboys and railroaders present, seemingly endeavoring to outbellow the carters.

Outside, Sanderson's exuberant night life was getting under way. In the railroad yards engines puffed, couplers banged, brake rigging clanged and jangled. Strings of cars rumbled down the gravity humps, lanterns waved, signal lights flashed from white to red or vice-versa. Cow ponies thudded their irons in the streets, and there was a continuous babble of voices.

Clag and Welch sauntered out, waving and nodding. And Slade was sure of the mocking gleam in Clag's eyes. And he had an unpleasant conviction that the sardonically amused glitter was not only for past performance but a repeat in the near future.

What? He had a fairly good idea as to what, but not dying. Got two hours' start on us, but rm depending on the slightest idea, at the moment, what to do about it. Well, all he could do was await developments. Perhaps they would provide the lead he sorely needed.

They would!

However, if Clag had something planned, he did not at once put it into effect. The night wore on quietly, quietly as Sanderson's nights ever did, and no reports of untoward happenings came in. Apparently the outlaws slept the sleep of the unjust. And next day Slade decided on a course of action.

He dropped in at the Sanderson bank for a gab with his old friend the president. After a little aimless chatter he asked a question.

'Chuck, has there been any money movement of late that you think might interest me?'

'Well, there was one this afternoon, although whether it will interest you or not I don't know. Haley Welch just about cleaned out his account — and it wasn't a small one — a couple of hours ago. Said he planned to invest in a couple of oil wells, that he was to meet with the owners in their office by the wells and close the deal. They wanted cash money. He stowed the dinero in a poke and said he was riding to Tumble. Headed that way, all right.'

'A couple of hours ago?' Slade repeated interrogatively.

'That's right.'

'Chuck,' Slade said, 'will you please get in touch with Crane right away and tell him to follow me to Tumble?'

'Sure, do it right away,' the president promised. 'What are you going to do, Walt?'

'I'm going to try and save a man's life,' *El Halcón* replied. 'I only hope I won't be too late.'

He was out the door before the banker could ask questions.

Reaching Shadow's stable, Slade cinched up without a moment's delay and said:

'Once again, feller, it's up to you keep a good man from you and I'm sure you'll make it! Let's go!'

Reaching the trail, he gradually increased the horse's pace until he was going at top speed. With care Slade scanned every thicket and hill crest and the trail ahead for what he most dreaded to see, a still form sprawled in the dust. He had a notion where the try would be made, not on the open prairie. But he knew he could be mistaken.

However, nowhere was there sign of life, nor of death. The trail stretched on and on through the glow of the westering sun, empty.

With only the upper rim of the sun showing above the horizon, he sighted the smoke smudge over the oil field. Another half hour, with the full dark closing down, and he reached Tumble.

At the edge of the field he drew rein and for a couple of moments sat at ease. Lerner had pointed out the two wells in question, which were rather close together but isolated from the other bores. There was a good-sized shack the two owners used for an office and where one sometimes slept.

Slade had studied the area and was familiar with its details. The shack had two doors, front and back. Opposite the front door and only a few yards distant was a straggle of brush broad enough and thick enough to hide men and horses at night. The approach to the back door was empty, nothing to provide concealment.

Dropping the split reins to the ground, Slade dismounted, patted Shadow's velvety neck. He eased around the edge of the field, avoiding the groups of workers, until he was in a position to make a dash for that back door.

Directly in line with the door, which stood partly open, he paused, scanning the terrain in every direction, his ears attuned to any alien sound that might seep through the clang and grumble of the field. He saw nothing, heard nothing.

Drawing a deep breath, he started on the perilous dash to the door.

It was a nerve-racking business, drifting across the open with the outlaws possibly holed up in the brush or approaching it. But he took some small comfort from the belief that the bulk of the shack would conceal his approach from inimical eyes.

As he neared the shack, with nothing happening, he heard a rumble of voices and an occasional laugh. Somebody in there, all right; several somebodies. With quick, light steps he covered the last few yards, flattened against the shack wall, and inched silently to where he could peer through the half-open door.

Sitting at a table, smoking and talking, were the two well owners and Haley Welch, whose money poke lay beside him on the table. Looked like his hunch was a straight one.

But as the slow minutes passed on leaden feet and nothing happened, he began to wonder uneasily if he had blundered some way and the try was not going to be made here.

Without the least preliminary warning, the front door banged open. Through it surged three men, two with neckerchiefs tied high, the third tall and bearded.

The masked outlaws held guns on Welch and the well owners. The bearded man seized the money poke and tucked it under his arm.

Slade leaped into the room. 'Trail's end, Clag!' he thundered. 'Up! You are under arrest! In the name of the State of Texas! Anything you say — '

With a howl of maniacal fury, Clag dropped the poke and went for his gun. He was fast, lightning fast, but *El Halcón* shaded him by the flicker of an eyelash. He reeled back and fell, his breast and lungs shattered by the Ranger's bullets.

His two companions were shooting at the weaving, ducking Ranger as fast as they could squeeze trigger. Welch leaped to his feet and over went the table, smashing into the owlhoots, giving Slade the instant of respite that was the difference between life and death.

Another moment and he lowered his smoking Colts to peer through the powder fog at the motionless forms sprawled on the floor. He walked slowly to where Bertram Clag, the outlaw leader, lay. He ripped the false beard free to disclose Clag's distorted features and held before his glazing eyes something he had slipped from a secret pocket in his broad leather belt — a gleaming silver star set on a silver circle, the feared and honored badge of the Texas Rangers! Clag's baleful glare fixed on the symbol of law and order and justice for all, and he died.

Slipping the badge back in its hiding place, Slade turned to the gibbering occupants of the room.

'Take it easy,' he said. 'Everything is under control. There's your money on the floor, Welch. Put it back in the bank and don't fall for any more loco yarns about deep oil pools. There is none here; all the geological indications are against such a thing, as Westbrook Lerner will tell you. Clag made up that fairy tale to further his own outlaw activities. Knowing, too, that sooner or later he'd beguile some trusting soul into packing along money to invest in his mythical wells.'

'He sure fooled me,' Welch sighed. 'Although toward the last I was beginning to feel a little funny about him, somehow.'

'Which I think he sensed,' Slade said, adding grimly, 'and because of which I don't think he would have let you leave this room alive.' Welch shuddered.

'Guess we don't need to be asking Lerner questions,' put in one of the well owners. 'If Mr. Slade says it's so, it is so. '

'Thank you' Slade acknowledged. 'And thank you, Haley, for shoving that table over when you did; it came in handy.'

'Was a plumb accident,' the carter replied sheepishly. 'I hit it with my knees when I jumped out of my chair.'

The shooting had been heard, and men were poking cautious heads in the door, bawling questions.

'Come in and we'll tell you about it,' Slade invited. 'First, though, will somebody please locate Deputy Blount and fetch him here. Tell him to leave word for Sheriff Crane, who should be reaching town any minute now.'

A couple of men hurried off to take care of the chore. Slade regaled the others with a brief summary of the affair and some of the things that led up to it. Followed much clucking and shaking of heads. With exclaimings over Bertram Clag's perfidy and the way he had had everybody fooled.

'That is, everybody except Mr. Slade,' somebody said. 'Don't nobody fool him.'

The deputy arrived shortly. 'Met him on the way,' explained the man who had been sent to fetch him.

'When I heard the shooting over here I knew darn well what was going on,' Blount said. 'Got here as quick as I could. Left word at Branding Pen Two for Sheriff Tom. Wouldn't be surprised if he comes straight here, too.'

The sheriff did put in an appearance in short order, and didn't appear surprised at what had happened. With him was Mary Merril.

'Of course I rode along with him when Uncle Tom told me you had gallivanted this way, leaving word for him to follow you,' she said. 'Thank heaven you're all right, but I see I've got another chore of patching your shirt and overalls. You're sure none of those slugs touched you?'

After receiving a brief review of the happening, the sheriff said:

'And that takes care of one of the worst outlaw bunches we ever had to contend with. Now maybe we can have a mite of peace and quiet for a spell. That is, until some other hellion pops up.'

'If one does, just send for Mr. Slade,' he was advised.

'A notion,' Crane agreed. 'Okay, some of you gents please pack the carcasses to my office and put 'em on the floor.'

Which was done, Blount going along to superintend the chore. Slade, the sheriff, and Mary headed for Branding Pen Two and much-needed food.

'Listen to those hellions at the bar giving Clag what-for,' snorted Crane. 'Yesterday they couldn't say enough good about him.'

'The way of the world,' Slade replied cheerfully. 'When the baron is defeated, the serfs came out of their holes in the castle rock and fling their curses across the moat. The way of the world; always was and always will be.'

'Well, at least we can really relax for a few days now,' Mary said thankfully.

★　★　★

Several days later she said:

'Hurry back, dear; you'll need me to patch up your shirts and overalls.'

With laughter on her lips, but tears on her lashes, she watched him ride away, tall and graceful atop his great black horse, the late sunshine etching his sternly handsome profile in flame, to where duty called and new adventure waited.